THE MONTAUK MYSTERY

THE MONTAUK MYSTERY

•

Diane Sawyer

AVALON BOOKS
NEW YORK

PRINTED IN THE UNITED STATES OF AMERICA
ON ACID-FREE PAPER
BY HADDON CRAFTSMEN, BLOOMSBURG, PENNSYLVANIA

To my husband Robert, for his love and understanding

To Kirk and Linda Sawyer, and to Barrie and Luis Bonaventura, for their encouragement, love and enthusiasm.

To Colin Sawyer,
for helping me to see the world as an exciting place filled with adventure.

To Grace Murdock and Peggy Nolan, gracious and talented St. Petersburg writers, for their advice and continued interest in my work.

To those family members and friends who listened to my ideas and read my stories.

And last, but not least, to Veronica Mixon, editor at Avalon Books, for her helpful suggestions which turned my manuscript into a publishable novel.

Chapter One

"**B**rrrrr!" Shrugging off the chilly March air, Annie Devane pushed her suitcase through the doorway of the Corner Cafe. She tossed her red beret and sweater onto a peg and shook loose her dark curls. The bus to take her back to the State University at Albany wouldn't be along for another hour.

"Hi, everybody," Annie called to the eleven-o'clock regulars. Mostly retirees and shop owners, who sat at tables in groups of two and three, they greeted Annie with raised cigarettes and coffee cups.

"Hey, Annie, come sit at the counter," Sally, the waitress, said. "I'll give the regulars another caffeine fix, then we'll talk."

Annie liked the down-home feeling of the Corner Cafe. Situated at the intersection of Main and Front Streets, it was the hub of local news in Grayrocks, a

1

resort town on the eastern tip of Long Island. Annie turned halfway around on her stool and rested her elbows on the counter. She listened to the conversation that drifted her way.

Nell, a regular who commandeered the corner table, was saying, "This new guy in town, this Matt Revington, he's trouble. Have you seen how he roars around in that fancy convertible? Guns the engine at every traffic light. Just yesterday he cut off my cousin on Shore Road."

Ed's nasal voice interrupted. "According to the barbershop guys, Matt's in town to finalize plans to work at his uncle David's marina."

"Everyone in the pool-hall crowd's placing bets on how long the greenhorn will last," Jake added.

Nell chuckled. "Day one's favored to win. Day seven's a long shot."

Ed said, "Matt's daddy thought he was too good for this town. He took his share of the family's fortune and moved to a ritzy high-rise in New York City. Now he's sending us his son." He threw up his hands. "What did we do to deserve another Revington?"

Annie wasn't surprised to hear the regulars badmouth the Revingtons. This was Grayrocks, where a "them" versus "us" mentality ruled. In high season, "them" meant rich tourists who asked dumb questions about swimming, boating, and fishing while working on their tans. During low season, "them" referred to rich locals, like the Revingtons, who never dirtied their hands making a living. The Revingtons claimed they invested in real-estate ventures. The general opinion was that the Revingtons had been grabbing other people's land for centuries, dating back to when the Montauk Indians were driven from the area.

"Look, Annie," Sally said. "There's Matt Revington across the street, on the corner. Wonder what he's up to."

Annie turned and saw a tall, lanky guy in his early twenties leaning against a doorway, his hands shoved deep into his pockets. "He's the one causing all this commotion?" she asked. She watched Matt cross the street in long, easy strides.

Mabel, who occupied a booth along the window, said, "Way I hear it, young Revington was sent to schools out west. Now he's come back east to prove himself on the old family stomping grounds. His daddy's threatening to cut him out of his will." Mabel caught Annie's eye. "Stay away from that one, Annie Devane. He's not your type. He'll never amount to anything."

Annie laughed. "Romance? No way. Painting and photography, that's what's on my mind."

"He doesn't look much like a rich guy in that jacket and jeans," Sally remarked.

Annie peered through the window. "What's with the reflector sunglasses and cowboy hat? I wonder where he thinks he's going."

Ed looked up from his coffee. "He's probably headed to Slim's Auto Shop. I hear he had some work done on that red Corvette 360 of his. Probably wants to outshine every stud in these parts. He'd better save up that loose energy for when he starts work at his uncle's marina this May. The crew out there has a few surprises ready for him."

"Hey, he's coming here," Sally said to Annie. "Whoa, isn't he one good-looking hunk of flesh and bones?"

Matt Revington pushed open the door and walked to the counter. He stopped next to Annie and slung his leg over the stool. "Good mornin', ma'am," he said to Sally. "May I see a menu?"

Annie liked his Texas drawl and husky voice. She couldn't help but notice his roguish good looks.

The regulars disguised their snickers with coughs as Sally rapped her knuckles on the blackboard. "This here's our menu," she said.

Matt unzipped his suede jacket. "I'll need a few minutes to check out the specials," he drawled.

From the corner of her eye, Annie noticed the green and black designs on his T-shirt. She inched forward and read the words: "Indy 500."

Sally leaned toward Matt as she tightened her ponytail. The dark roots along the center part widened. "How would you like our special, big boy?" She fluttered her eyelashes, perfecting the blond-bombshell act she had first performed in a red sequin gown at the Senior Talent Show. Back then, Annie was an impressionable eighth-grader. She had considered Sally, her next-door neighbor, the most glamorous person in the world, a future star passing through Grayrocks on her way to Hollywood.

Matt stared hard into Sally's eyes but said nothing.

"Well," Sally said, and walked away in a huff. "Aren't you something."

Annie knew that lots of first-timers, caught off guard by Sally's brazen act, came back with a wisecrack to save face. But Matt had chosen silence.

Sally turned back to face Matt. She smiled, obviously paving the way for a good tip. "Why don't you try the clam chowder. We're famous for it."

Matt leaned toward Annie. He smiled a brilliant smile, showing even white teeth. Creases formed in his tanned cheeks, accentuating his high cheekbones. His aquiline nose enhanced his brawny, rugged appearance. "Do you eat the chowder here, ma'am?" he asked.

Annie's heart raced. "Only if my health and fire insurance are paid up." She didn't need eyes in the back of her head to know her reply would bring grins and thumbs-up signals from the regulars. She was born and bred in Grayrocks. She knew how to play Get the Outsider.

"Thanks, Annie," he said. "I'll take out those policies later. For now, I'll take my chances. Serve up that chowder, ma'am."

Surprised, Annie blurted out, "How do you know my name?"

Before answering, Matt removed his sunglasses. Annie looked into his gorgeous eyes, as blue as the waters off Midnight Point. *Snap out of this,* she told herself. *Rich guy, poor girl, two different worlds, lots of heartache.* She forced herself to remember all those tragic stories of town girls ridiculed and eventually rejected by the East Bay Country Club set. She knew better. Every girl in Grayrocks knew better. But still, there was no denying that those blue eyes were gorgeous.

"My uncle told me about you," Matt replied. "He described you and said you'd be here waiting for the noontime bus to Albany. He bragged that you're a very talented photographer and artist. He said you won several awards at college. That's why I'm here. I have a project you might be interested in."

Project? A warning bell went off in Annie's head. Anytime a Revington mentioned the word *project,* watch out! He wanted your land or your neighbor's or your relative's. Well, Matthew Revington wasn't going to finagle her gram out of their Baywatch Inn. No way!

He smiled warmly. "Let me introduce myself. I'm Matt Revington."

"Our finest," Sally said, setting a steaming bowl of chowder in front of Matt. "And something to nibble on until it cools." She dumped a handful of oyster crackers into a saucer.

Matt continued: "Why don't you let me drive you back to the university? I can explain the photography project. It's perfect for you."

"Photography project?" Annie's green eyes opened wide.

"I'm giving you the chance to take on an interesting art project. You could add it to your résumé."

Matt tasted the chowder and hungrily downed several spoonfuls.

"I'd like to hear a few details," Annie said. She would proceed cautiously. The Revingtons didn't understand the principle of give-and-take. They took, but they never gave. There would be strings attached.

"It's a six-hour ride to Albany. Why not come along with me? We'd have plenty of time to discuss the project." He savored the last spoonful of chowder. "I can tell you this much. It's a great opportunity to work with a very professional team."

"Art and photography, you said?"

"Yes, ma'am."

"Will there be anything else?" Sally asked.

"No, thank you, ma'am." Matt stood up in a slow, unwinding motion and dug his wallet out of his back pocket. "Just the check and I'll be leaving."

"My check too," Annie said. "Matt's driving me back to school." She slung her purse over her shoulder and reached for her suitcase.

"Let me get that," Matt said, taking the suitcase from Annie's hands.

Matt gasped as the suitcase banged against his leg. "What's in there, rocks?" He stumbled and grabbed the counter.

"Yes," Annie said, suppressing a smile. "Along with some other Grayrocks beach stuff, for an art project."

Sally came from behind the counter and hugged Annie. "I'll miss you. I'm sorry we never got together this week. Between this job and the way things are at home, I'm lucky if I can find time to breathe. Are we still best friends?"

"Sure. Forever." Annie remembered that blustery day five years ago at the cemetery overlooking Grayrocks Bay. She had placed carnations on her parents' caskets and sobbed in Sally's arms. "Best friends forever," Annie said softly. "You and Gram Jenkins got me through some tough times. I'll never forget that." They hugged again.

Annie knew that all eyes were focused on her and Matt. They would be the talk of the Corner Café for the next hour. "Good-bye," she said, waving to everyone. "See you this summer."

Up came the cigarettes and coffee cups in a farewell salute.

At the doorway, Matt sneezed several times.

Sally remarked, "Allergic to the working class?"

"No, ma'am," Matt replied. "Matter of fact, I hope to be joining the Grayrocks working class very soon."

Matt was hit by another attack of sneezing. "How much pepper do they put in the chowder?" he asked Annie.

"Just part of the Grayrocks welcoming ceremony," Annie said. She caught the regulars' knowing looks. They were saying, *We'll show newcomers who's in control around here.*

Annie passed through the doorway beneath Matt's arm. Outside in the chilly mist, she noticed again the flash of his brilliant smile. She didn't know why, but she blushed and looked away.

Chapter Two

"Great day for a drive with the top down," Matt shouted to Annie as he revved up the engine. The storm that had threatened all morning retreated. Sunshine broke through gray clouds, creating lacework patterns of light on the buildings and sidewalks. Matt drove along Main Street, followed Soundview Highway along the shoreline of Long Island Sound, made fairly good time on New York 25, then entered the Long Island Expressway. Traffic inched along. It would take more than the usual three hours to travel Long Island's one-hundred-mile length.

As Matt drove, Annie noticed his long, lean thigh muscles that strained against his jeans and the firm grasp of his large, callused hands on the wheel. Those hands were familiar with hard work. She

9

imagined him on horseback herding cattle somewhere out west.

Each time he looked at her an odd sensation fluttered in her midsection. She felt strongly attracted to him and, at the same time, startled by the attraction. In high school, she'd gone out a few times with Nell's son, Doug, and to the senior prom with Ed's son, Junior. In college, she'd dated several guys, but no one had captured her heart. Falling in love was not in her plans. She wanted a career as an illustrator in the publishing world of New York City. However, now she was sitting next to Matt Revington, unable to subdue the butterflies that skittered around in her stomach.

"Tell me about the photography project," Annie said. She leaned back in the black leather seat. Welcoming the sun's warmth on her face, she pushed back the red beret that capped her dark curls.

"The truth is, I need your help."

"Tell me what you have in mind."

"I'd like you to work with me this summer. A team of archaeologists from Andrews University has hired me and my uncle's charter boat. They want to explore some islands near Grayrocks in search of Indian artifacts. They asked me to select an assistant."

"What islands?" She felt a tinge of pride that scientists from Long Island's prestigious Andrews University, near New York City, were interested in islands so close to her hometown.

"Big Shell and Little Shell Islands."

Annie gulped. The Shell Islands were parklands.

Developers wanted to build on them. Environmentalists wanted to protect them. Many people figured the Revingtons would find a way to add them to their holdings. But surely archaeologists from Andrews University wouldn't go along with a land-grabbing scheme. She wouldn't let her suspicions run wild. She would listen carefully to everything Matt said.

"Just those two islands?" she asked.

"Yes, ma'am. Only the uninhabited islands. The team has a two-month grant to explore them."

"What do they expect to find?

"They hope to dig up arrowheads, tools, pottery. Anything that will put together a profile of Indian life."

"They're a few hundred years too late," Annie said. "Anything the Indians left behind disappeared long ago. Kids have been exploring those islands for years. The library and school have display cases filled with artifacts. So do the museums in Northport and Riverhead."

"The team knows that sites have been disturbed," Matt said. "But they're hoping to find things that were overlooked."

"I don't think they'll have much luck."

Matt scoffed. "That's what people told Christopher Columbus and his crew."

Annie laughed. "And they discovered America. So, okay, maybe you'll discover something too. Gold and silver? Buried treasure? Who knows what!" She laughed again.

"You have a very active imagination," Matt said.

His curt tone unnerved her. So did his startled look, like a kid caught with his hands in the cookie jar. Had she accidentally stumbled onto something? Was Matt really looking for arrowheads on the Shell Islands? Or was there something else?

Matt's stony silence finally got to Annie. "I'm sorry," she said. "My comments were out of line."

"No, you were only kidding," he said. "I took offense because I don't like the expedition trivialized. It's not about gold and silver." Determination shone in his eyes. "There are things in this world more important than money."

He checked the rearview mirror. "Let's get back to business. The archaeologists asked me to find someone who knows the area and its legends. Someone with artistic ability and photographic experience . . . who could handle certain other jobs, too."

He sounded evasive, almost mysterious. "What other jobs?"

"You'd be responsible for labeling soil samples and entering data into a laptop computer." He turned toward her. "I figured you and the Shells had a very special bond. I thought you'd jump at the chance to work there."

Matt shifted to the other lane. "Uncle David told me about the Save Our Shells Committee, the S.O.S., I believe you call it. He mentioned that your mother was elected the first president of the S.O.S. but died before she had a chance to serve. He said your grandmother is the current president. And I heard that when you were only fourteen, you helped your parents design the first S.O.S. poster."

Annie fought the lump that formed in her throat whenever she thought about her parents and the accident that took their lives. "I could be interested in the project," she said.

"Some of the work will be physically difficult. It'll take a joint effort to pack up supplies, lug ice chests filled with food in and out of the boat, and set up tents." He took one hand off the wheel and squeezed the muscle in her upper arm. "Are you strong enough?"

"I can pull my own weight," she replied. She was caught off guard by the warm, tingling feeling in her arm where he touched her.

"Glad to hear it," he said. "Andrews University has a sizable grant and a fair amount of money to pay us. They'll expect you to earn your way. I'll be counting on you too."

The muscles in Matt's face tensed. Annie sensed there was more to this expedition than he cared to tell. Maybe he wasn't going after buried treasure, but there was something valuable at stake. She remembered the talk in the Corner Cafe, something about one last chance to prove himself before being cut off from the Revington money. Matt claimed that this expedition wasn't about money, but she wasn't going to fall for that line. He was a Revington, after all. She would be patient. The real reason would eventually jump up, like fish for bait worms.

"Oh, by the way," he said, a smile returning to his

face. "My uncle suggested that your grandmother could help us with the menus and prepare the same food she serves at Baywatch Inn. It pays well."

Annie knew that the extra money would allow Gram to make a dream come true. She wanted to add an apartment over the garages at Baywatch Inn. "I need a hideaway from the tourists," Gram always said. But Annie knew that Gram really wanted to provide Sally and her boys with a place to stay in case her marriage to Tom ended. Sally, who over-looked Tom's cruelties, claimed he needed tender loving care. Annie thought he was just plain mean. His nastiness frightened her.

"I think that could be worked out," Annie said, squinting into the afternoon sun. "I'll talk to Gram." She laughed. "Hey! This means I can quit my exciting summer job at the cannery." She wrinkled her nose at the memory of fish chowder pouring into cans.

Matt laughed. His smile was warm and friendly.

Annie laced her fingers behind her head and thought about working with Matt. One serious drawback struck her. "We need to clear the air about something."

"I know what's coming," Matt said. "You're afraid people will say Annie Devane's slaving away for a Revington, the enemy."

"I know how stupid that sounds." Annie sighed. "But you didn't grow up in Grayrocks."

"No, but my uncle David and aunt Arabelle warned me that the people of Grayrocks have despised the Revington name for centuries. It's too bad that a bright person like you would believe everything you hear without getting the facts straight."

Annie's cheeks burned with indignation. "You certainly seem to know everything. Go ahead, give me the facts. We have plenty of time."

"Okay," Matt said defiantly. "Fact. The Revington family immigrated to Long Island in the sixteen hundreds. Fact. Like many of this country's founding fathers, they acquired their fortune by speculating in land, not stealing it . . ."

Annie held up her hand. "Stop right there. The Revingtons bought up the land claims of discouraged settlers real cheap. Then they turned around and sold the claims for huge profits. It's called greed."

"It's called good business," Matt said.

"Hah! The Revingtons practically stole land claims from the Indians."

Matt shook his head. "My relatives abided by the law. Their land purchases were approved by whatever Englishman had jurisdiction. That's more than can be said for many unscrupulous real-estate wheeler-dealers back then. Didn't you ever put down your paintbrushes long enough to study history? England's James the First granted a near empire in the New World, including these lands, to the earl of Sterling and other influential men."

Annie's eyes glinted intently. "Let's talk about *this* century. During Prohibition, the Revingtons were bootleggers."

"Who wasn't? Grayrocks had speakeasies and gin

mills. There were false-bottom trucks and schooners everywhere. My relatives supplied the land where the bootleggers built warehouses and wharves."

Annie huffed. "Revingtons are opportunists."

"Give me facts to back up that accusation." Matt spoke through clenched teeth.

"Here's a fact," Annie retorted. "When the Revingtons got wind that the Long Island Railroad Company planned to lay tracks from New York City to Grayrocks, they grabbed that strip of land so fast, it made heads spin."

Matt sputtered, "They were visionaries."

"Visionaries?" Annie fumed. "Right now they're probably envisioning how to grab land from the poorer families in Grayrocks."

"What are you talking about?"

"Everybody knows if the word *foreclosure* is even hinted at, the Revingtons step in."

Matt turned toward Annie, fire in his eyes. "Obviously you've been getting your information from that loafing element that's been hanging around the Corner Cafe for generations. If they spent as much time working as they did bad-mouthing my family, they'd be rich by now."

"Spoken like a true Revington," Annie said, glaring at him.

Matt pounded the steering wheel. "In case you've forgotten, when times were tough, Revington money backed small businesses with low-interest loans and provided employment." He shook his head. "My uncle David and aunt Arabelle are treated like snobs who came by their money illegally and effortlessly. It's unfair. How would you like it if your parents had been accused of overcharging customers at their photography shop?"

Annie balled her hands into tight fists. "How dare you!" she shouted. "My parents were honest, hard-working people."

"But they weren't rich. So no one bothered to invent rumors about them." He spat out the words. "Roll that around in your head for a while."

Annie seethed with anger. She was sorry she had ever met Matt Revington. She couldn't wait to get to Albany. She didn't say a word for the next half hour as she tried to simmer down. Staring out the window, mulling over Matt's words, she applied Gram's advice: Try to see things from both points of view.

Annie's logical nature fought with her emotions. She had to admit that Matt stood up for his family. And rumors did have a way of turning into facts, especially when the rumors were about the Revingtons. Besides, if Matt was part of a legitimate archaeological expedition and she wasn't being pulled into some Revington scheme, then she had nothing to lose and very much to gain. "This fighting won't get us anywhere," she said finally.

Matt breathed deeply and exhaled. "But it certainly cleared the air."

They both laughed.

Matt looked away from the road, into her eyes. "Let's agree to cooperate. Deal?" He offered his hand.

"Deal." She shook his broad, rugged hand. He smiled and turned his attention to the road. For the second time that day, Annie reminded herself that rich guys were out of her league. She wasn't about to invite pain and humiliation into her life. *Think of Matt as a business partner,* she told herself. Nothing more. Just a business partner.

Chapter Three

Annie looked at her watch. She and Matt had been traveling four hours. They were making good time on the Taconic Parkway, a major route from New York City to Albany. "Working together should be interesting," Annie said. "We have nothing in common."

"Sure we do."

"Like what?" she asked.

"You're an only child. So am I."

"That's not much."

"I heard that you skipped a grade in school and graduated at sixteen and that you're a straight-A student at Albany." He paused. "I got an A once. In kindergarten, for nap-taking skills."

Annie laughed. She enjoyed Matt's easygoing ways. She studied his unmistakable Revington profile, his prominent nose, high cheekbones, slightly jutting chin. He wore his thick black hair longer than most Grayrocks men. *Maybe he's got Indian blood running through his veins,* she thought. She blinked away the image of Matt riding bareback on a horse, his bow and arrow poised, ready to attack the enemy, his face streaked with red and black war paint.

"You're taking quite a chance," she said. "You really don't know anything about my paintings or photographs. What did your uncle tell you?"

"Actually it's my aunt Arabelle who offered good references."

"That's impossible," Annie blurted out. "Arabelle Revington is the—"

"The recluse of Grayrocks." Matt finished her sentence. "I know the label they've pinned on her."

"We've never met," Annie said. She stopped short of saying we travel in different circles.

"My aunt Arabelle says you're very talented, Annie. She likes your watercolors best."

"That's hard to believe." Annie's voice turned sharp. "Your aunt Arabelle doesn't know me. She's never spoken to me. Nor has your uncle David."

"You may be surprised to know that Aunt Arabelle owns one of your paintings."

"Really?" Annie's eyebrows shot up.

"Sea Treasures," he replied.

"But that was sold at my college, at an exhibition last year."

"A friend went on Aunt Arabelle's behalf. At Aunt

Arabelle's insistence, she selected that one. Apparently it held some special meaning for her."

Why would Sea Treasures *appeal to Arabelle Revington?* Annie wondered. She had painted it on bright sunny days in July, the first summer after her parents died. To fight off the black despair of grief, she had worked in the broiling sun, surrounded by whiteness. She had felt better as she captured on canvas the blinding white sand, the sand castles and seashells baking in the sun's blistering rays, the solitary starfish reaching its arms in all directions. Many browsers commented on the loneliness of the painting, which depicted footprints but no people. When Annie overheard a freckle-faced boy say, "The people disappeared into the sunset," only then did she feel as if she had put the past behind her, and in a beautiful resting place.

"Your painting makes Aunt Arabelle sad. She's haunted by it."

Tears welled in Annie's eyes and threatened to overflow. "I'm glad *Sea Treasures* found a good home and someone who appreciates it." She turned away so that Matt wouldn't see her dab her eyes with a tissue.

Matt continued, oblivious to her sniffles. "Dr. Winfield, who heads up the archaeology team, is the father of Dan Winfield, my old college roommate. In Texas," he added, pointing to his cowboy hat, which sat between them. "I've known Dr. Winfield for six years. He's a scholarly man, dedicated to his field.

He can be overbearing and bossy when there's work to be done, but you'll grow to like him."

Annie couldn't squelch her curiosity. "I don't understand why you would take on this job."

"I hate to admit it, but I've made some mistakes and I've been an irresponsible son. My father thinks I'll never make anything of myself. But Uncle David convinced him to give me a last chance." He looked in the rearview mirror, then changed lanes. "If I don't make any mistakes this summer, my father promised to back my plans to become a professional race-car driver."

"And you're counting on me, someone you only met today, to help you. That's strange."

The muscles in his face tightened. "I thought you, of all people, might understand. My uncle told me about the automobile accident that took your parents from you, and I'm sorry to hear about your loss. But I also know that you've pulled your life together. You're a survivor. You fight for what you want. You know how to turn things around."

Annie was moved by his words. She and Matt came from very different worlds, but they did have things in common, after all. "If we're going to work together, I should know more about you," she said.

He thought for several minutes. "I'm a guy who appreciates speed. I want to tear up the highways with a motorcycle, roar a stockcar around a track. I like to race a speedboat at full throttle, skydive, hang glide, you name it. Mostly, I want to win the Indy

Five Hundred before I turn twenty-four, the Le Mans before I'm twenty-five."

Annie could feel the excitement build in Matt as he spoke. A reckless, untamed streak ran through him. It made her jittery.

Suddenly, Matt floored the gas pedal. The car roared down the parkway, weaving in and out of traffic. Annie leaned forward and grabbed the dashboard.

Matt turned and saw the terror in her eyes. "What's wrong?" he asked.

"I'm not riding with you if you're going to drive like this," she cried, unable to quell her panic.

"I'm sorry," he said. He released his foot. "I should have realized that driving fast would upset you."

Annie tried to calm herself, but her heart beat wildly. Ever since she had survived the accident that killed her parents, she'd been terrified of speed. She would never allow herself to fall for someone who recklessly toyed with death. She pictured motorcycles spinning out of control, speedboats careening into the air, race cars bursting into flames.

"Annie," Matt said. "I'm really sorry. I love to race against the wind. It gives me a tremendous feeling of freedom, but I wouldn't do anything to upset you. I want us to get along. Never again, I promise."

The sincerity of his words touched Annie's heart. "We're still partners," she said quietly. *Matt Revington. Rich guy, racer. That's two strikes against him,* Annie decided. Would there be a third?

As they drove on in silence, Annie began to have

doubts about her ability to handle the summer work. "I hope we're not getting in over our heads," she admitted. "I don't know much about archaeology. Do you?"

"A little. I have a master's degree in archaeology from the University of Texas."

Annie's eyes opened wide. "I thought from the calluses on your hands you rustled cattle in the Wild West."

"No, ma'am. I worked for a while on a dude ranch. But mainly I've been hauling rocks at an archaeological dig."

"Did you uncover anything interesting?"

"Not much," he said. "Indians are good at covering their tracks."

As they talked, Annie sensed Matt's admiration for the Indians of eastern Long Island, a confederation of thirteen tribes, each with its own name. Collectively they called themselves Montauks, because their sachem, their grand chief, lived at Montauk Point.

Matt said, "You'll need to research the Montauks, especially the Shinnecock and Manhasset tribes. Your college library will have information."

Annie wasn't surprised that Matt had named the Manhassets. They had inhabited the Shell Islands. "Why the Shinnecocks?" she asked.

"Their descendants still live on the four-hundred-acre reservation in Southampton. The governor deeded it to them in 1703, back when the English and Dutch were fighting over Long Island. Dr. Winfield thinks the Shinnecocks might help us. They're an ancient people. Carbon dating traces bones from their grave sites to 1290 B.C. And they're a proud people who want to preserve their history."

Annie vowed to learn as much as she could about the Montauks. She didn't like Matt knowing more about Long Island people and places than she did.

"Don't overlook any aspect of research on the Montauks," Matt continued. "The team expects you to be knowledgeable. Besides, as an artist, you'll appreciate the Montauks' wampum designs. They're the best." He leaned forward and gripped the wheel tightly. "If, by chance during your research, you find any wampum designs that refer to the Shell Island, call me at my uncle's marina. Right away."

"Okay."

"Promise?"

"Yes, of course," she said, surprised by his intensity.

"Come to think of it," he said, "if anything about the wampum designs reminds you, in any way, of the Shell Islands, call me."

"Okay," she said emphatically.

He smiled. "Give free reign to your woman's intuition. Your artist's instincts too." He changed lanes abruptly. "There's no reason to mention the details of our expedition, or of your research, to anyone."

She laughed. "You're making this sound like a secret mission."

"In a way it is," he said. "Grant money is hard to obtain. We don't want people from your university, or elsewhere, to get in the way of the Andrews University team." He cleared his throat. "Don't forget, study the wampum designs every chance you get. If anyone gets curious, say it's for an art project."

The urgency in Matt's voice startled Annie. The wampum designs were very important to him. Suddenly they seemed like the focal point of the expedition.

Matt said, "I thought of another thing. You need to join a spelunkers' club at school."

Annie shot him a quizzical look.

"That's right. We'll be exploring the caves on Big and Little Shell. You need to be prepared."

Annie smiled. Matt was still the outsider who had much to learn. There were only a few small caves and only one large enough to stand in. It was located on Big Shell Island, and it contained nothing more than rats' nests, bird droppings, and candy wrappers left behind by kids who played there during family camping trips.

"Okay, Matt," she teased. "I'll join a spelunkers' club, and just for you I'll learn the ropes."

"This is serious business, Annie. The success of the team's efforts could very well depend on your familiarity with the ropes." His intensity intrigued her. Something powerful, something passionate, motivated him. Whatever it was, it was located on the Shells. And she wanted to be there when he found it.

Matt continued: "I'd like to scout out those caves on the Shells right away. But I'll wait until we have our team assembled. I hope we don't attract too much attention, bring up too many questions, from, uh, certain people."

"You mean the All-Atlantic Associates?" Annie asked.

Matt nodded.

Bitterness crept into Annie's voice. "They and others like them have been hovering around Grayrocks like vultures long before my parents formed S.O.S. When time runs out next year on the Shells' park status, they plan to buy up the land and fill it with condos." Annie stopped short. She regretted being so open. If rumors held any weight, Matt's family had their own plans for the Shell Islands. But then, she realized, Matt's uncle would have already told Matt about every piece of property in and around Grayrocks. She wasn't revealing anything he didn't already know.

"I've heard about the All-Atlantic Associates, but I've never met any of them," Matt said. "Have you?"

"No. But I heard about their greedy, underhanded activities. For months before my parents died, Long Island environmental groups called our home day and night. They warned my parents—my mother was the newly elected president then—that All-Atlantic Associates would try to bypass certain laws about designated parklands."

Matt's eyes narrowed in a fierce squint. "Maybe something will turn up during our exploration that will stop the All-Atlantic Associates dead in their tracks."

Annie liked Matt's optimism and fighting spirit,

although she knew it wouldn't help. For years, Gray-rocks civic leaders had met to discuss the soon-to-be-defunct parkland status of the Shell Islands. But national agencies were not interested in the tiny islands. State and county agencies lacked authority to do anything.

"Matt, while I'm going to spelunker-club meetings and researching the Montauks, you should study Grayrocks's tides and currents."

"Looks like we both have homework," he said. They laughed together like two happy conspirators.

"We're here," Annie announced. In the semidarkness, the gray stone buildings of the State University loomed ahead of them. "There's Bradford Hall." She pointed toward one of four buildings overlooking a grassy lawn where a volleyball game was in progress under the lights.

Matt turned toward Annie. "I'd like to stay in touch between now and when we begin work. I might have some questions."

"Good idea," she said. "There's lots to organize. I finish here the third week in May."

"We won't have much time," he said. "Our first expedition is scheduled for the first weekend in June."

"That'll be the most important one," Annie added. "You know, first impressions."

"Yes," he said, "they last a lifetime."

Matt had a gorgeous smile, there was no denying that, Annie admitted. She wrote her phone number on a piece of paper and handed it to him.

Grabbing her suitcase with both hands, Matt pulled it from the pit. "I'm curious about what you'll do with this pile of rocks," he said, struggling toward the dorm.

"It's going to be a collage, a humorous look at the Grayrocks beaches." She thought for a moment. "I'll try to work the Montauk Indians and their wampum designs into the project. You know, to avoid any suspicion about why I'm doing all kinds of research in the library instead of partying with my friends."

Matt held her gaze. "You'll find tragedy, not humor, when you see what happened to the Montauk Indians." His brooding eyes and melancholy look startled her.

Annie watched Matt back out of the parking lot. A wave of sadness swept over her. It wasn't only that she hated good-byes. It was more than that. She regretted Matt's desire to be a race driver. She regretted the irreparable chasm that social status created. There were too many obstacles for her to ever become involved with him.

Chapter Four

March. April. May. The semester had flown by, ending in a flurry of art projects, exams, and term papers. Now, savoring the evening breeze that rippled through Grayrocks and stirred her bedroom curtains, Annie realized how glad she was to be home.

Gram's perky voice traveled up the stairway. "Annie, come down and tell me more about these Indian sketches of yours. I've never seen so many shells."

Annie pictured Gram hunched over the dining-room table, studying the sketches. There were shells sketched everywhere—beneath every tree, next to every wigwam and tanning rack, around every corncrib and husking bin. Shells lined the berry patches and cornfields. Women piled them. Men drilled them. Children tossed lances at piles of shells and shot at them with long, thin blowguns.

"I'll just be a few minutes," Annie called out as she hefted her suitcase onto her bed. She dug out her paintbrushes and charcoal pencils and set them on her desk. After tossing her T-shirts on the closet shelf, she poked through her sneakers and sandals. Which ones were suitable for the expedition to the Shell Islands? In one week she'd be going there with Matt.

Matt. Matthew. His name made her heart flutter. The ringing of the telephone interrupted Annie's thoughts. Was it Matt? She remembered his first call. She was in her dorm working on her collage, *Beachtown USA*, arranging the seaweed, shells, and driftwood from Grayrocks Beach and feeling very homesick. She had blurted out, "I thought you disappeared into Grayrocks Bay."

"No, just my hat." He had chuckled. "The marina guys treated me to their special baptismal rites."

He had called her often and made her laugh with his account of the local news and shenanigans. She had tried to immerse herself in her studies, but often, too often, she caught herself daydreaming about him. One morning, seated at her easel, intending to complete a seascape, she absentmindedly mixed shades of blue paint on her palette and thought of Matt's eyes. And then, in her studio class, she picked up a brush, flexed the bristles against her fingers, and remembered Matt's thick black hair.

Annie unpacked her hiking boots and checked the laces for frayed areas. True to her word, she had joined a spelunkers' club. Although every muscle in her body ached after climbing the rugged cliffs near Albany, she enjoyed the challenge.

She set out a framed photo of Matt. Dressed in torn jeans and faded shirt, he was scraping barnacles off a boat. Surrounding him, Sally's husband, Tom, and the other marina guys flexed their muscles and mugged for the camera as they tossed Matt cans of varnish. Annie polished the silver frame with the tip of her shirt. She studied Matt's face. He didn't have the ruddy complexion and sun-bleached hair of many Grayrocks men who worked around boats and water. He stood out from the others. It wasn't just his looks. There was something different about him. A serenity. A oneness with his surroundings. An acceptance of the way things were.

Annie studied Matt's eyes. His fearless look affirmed that he jumped into new situations, eager to prove himself. Annie peered more closely at the photo. She could tell from the smiles on the guys' faces and the obvious horseplay that Matt fit in. A Revington accepted by the local population? That was hard to believe.

Something had disturbed her about Matt for quite some time. Something didn't ring true. It was as if he had calculated his every move since coming to Grayrocks in order to gain acceptance. He seemed to anticipate reactions, moving along a course he had set, accomplishing exactly what he wanted. He was a Revington. Revingtons controlled people. Matt's methods might differ from his uncle's and father's, but the results were the same. He got his way.

Was she being too skeptical? She had a habit of letting doubts pull her in different directions until she didn't know what to believe. According to Sally, Matt had won over the marina guys with hard work. Sally and Gram often telephoned. They raved about Matt.

Holding Matt's photo close to her heart, Annie flopped on the bed and remembered their calls:

"Matt's really a great guy," Sally said on one call. "He takes the boys fishing and crabbing. He took Tom, the boys, and me to Shell Island for a picnic."

"Don't know what I'd have done without Matt these past weeks," Gram told her on another call. "Yard work, repairs, you name it. My handyman decided to take his vacation. Left me high and dry, but Matt took care of everything. Sally tells me Matt's had coffee a few times at the Corner Cafe. Nell, Sam, and the other regulars are all warming up to him."

Sally called another time "Tom lost his job," she told Annie. "He was flirting with the new secretary at the marina when he should have been docking a boat. A tourist was crushed between the boat and the pilings. He's okay, a broken rib and some bruises, but it could have been real serious. Tom can't forgive himself.

"Matt comes by almost every evening. He and Tom work on fishing gear, the car, stuff like that. Matt won't give up on him. I think it's been a turning point for Tom."

On her most recent call, Sally told Annie, "Matt

put in a good word for Tom. He got his job back at the marina."

Annie remembered thinking that Matt was too good to be true. It was almost as if he were acting nice to Gram and Sally and Sally's family to impress her. Was he doing this so she wouldn't back out of the expedition? But why would he go to all that trouble to get her to the Shell Islands? What could possibly be waiting for them there?

Then, a week ago, during a telephone call from Sally, Annie had discovered that Matt wasn't so perfect, after all. He was a Revington through and through. He couldn't be believed or trusted. He had hardly finished sweet-talking her on the phone, as if she were the only one in the whole world who mattered, when Sally called. The words ran through her mind.

Sally: "Hi."

Tom's raspy voice had interrupted: "Annie, you better come home soon. All the gals for miles around are finding excuses to come to the marina and hang around Matt. I notice he goes for long hair and short skirts. He's been seen with a babe on his arm in every roadside inn from here to Riverhead."

Sally: "Just ignore Tom. He's teasing you. Matt's only dated once or twice that I know of. Nothing serious."

Annie had never known jealousy, but she had recognized it then as it stabbed her heart. She acknowledged it now as she sat up and tossed Matt's picture aside. "Men!" She huffed and turned her attention to her suitcases.

Annie rifled through her notebooks and set aside the ones labeled *Montauks.* As promised, she had spent hours in the library researching the Long Island Indians. It had turned into a labor of love. She was intrigued by the designs the Montauks created with the wampum beads they drilled from clamshells. Stringing the beads—some left natural white or purple, others dyed vivid colors—the Montauks created magnificent ceremonial strings and wampum belts. The colors and designs conveyed their messages.

Annie flipped through the photocopies she had made of ceremonial strings. A rainbow of colors jumped from the pages. Each ceremonial string was composed of several strands of beads, about three feet long, tied together at one end.

Gram knocked on the open door. "Thought you might like a cool drink." She strode across the room, her thick black braid bouncing across her yellow T-shirt. She handed Annie a glass of iced tea brimming with lemon slices and hopped onto the bed next to her.

"Thanks." Annie took a long, slow sip. "That hit the spot."

Gram leaned back on her elbows, hooked her thumbs in the belt loops of her jeans, and gazed at Annie. "Just now, poring over those photocopies, you reminded me of your mother. Caitlin would sit for hours, looking at her photographs, lost in her thoughts. What on earth are you looking at?"

Annie spread out several photocopies. "Ceremonial strings." She pointed to strings of purple beads. "The Montauks sent this to announce to neighboring tribes the death of a war chief." She pointed to another. "This blue and green one is my favorite. It's a Montauk fishermen's thank-you string to the Great Spirit for a large supply of fish."

"That's pretty," Gram said, singling out the one paper-clipped to pages of notes.

"It's a courtship string. A brave sent it to ask for a maiden's hand in marriage."

Gram winked. "I can guess why you're interested in courtship."

Flustered, Annie quickly gathered up the photocopies. She didn't want Gram to see Matt's initials entwined with hers in the doodles in the margins of the notes. "Wait until you see these," Annie said. She fanned out photocopies of wampum belts.

"They're huge!" Gram exclaimed.

"Some reached a length of six feet," Annie explained. "They contained as many as seven thousand beads. They were for very important events, like a peace treaty."

Gram shook her head. "What a shame you had to leave Grayrocks to learn about local history."

"I guess it's a chapter that many would like to forget."

"I smell hot blueberries," Gram said, bouncing off the bed. "My pies must be done." She hurried down the stairs, sandals flopping, as agile and energetic as a teenager. "Don't be long."

Annie's fingertips lingered on the beads as she pondered the fate of the artistic, hardworking Montauks. In their heyday, they harvested shells to make wampum beads for their own use. When stronger tribes and white men demanded wampum as tribute and used the beads as money, the Montauks were forced to slave away, cutting, rounding, drilling, and polishing shells with their stone implements. Their numbers declined, and in 1833 the few remaining Montauks migrated to Wisconsin.

The phone rang again.

"Annie!" Gram's voice echoed up the stairwell. "It's for you."

"Annie, how are you?" Matt asked. His husky voice took her breath away. "I'm really looking forward to seeing you."

"Same here." The words slipped out.

"That's good news," he said. There was a long pause. "Could I come over now?"

"Sure," she said. How stupid! Why hadn't she told him to come by in an hour? She was a mess. She scrambled around for her best shorts. Her hair was hopeless. Where were her good sandals? Every T-shirt she owned was paint-spattered or riddled with burn holes from the kilns in which she fired her ceramic creations.

A knock at the door. Annie hurried down the stairs. All her doubts about Matthew Revington flew out the window. "Come on in," she heard Gram say.

Moments later, Matt appeared carrying a small bouquet of daisies, Annie's favorite flower. He strode across the room. With his pale blue shirt neatly tucked into navy shorts, he was even more handsome than she remembered. His smile weakened her knees. His blue eyes held her captive. Why did he want to be a racer? Why couldn't he be an archaeologist? Why did he have to be a Revington? Why couldn't he be a Jones or a Smith?

"For you," Matt said as he pressed the flowers gently into Annie's hands.

She felt a warm sensation in her cheeks and realized she was blushing. "Thanks," she murmured.

Matt's gaze traveled over Annie's head and focused on the wall behind her.

"Wow!" he said, looking at her collage. "So this is *Beachtown USA*. The clams diving into bowls of chowder are really funny."

Gram plunked her hands on her slim hips. "Personally, I like the oysters on surfboards." She leaned back and squinted. "The lobsters sipping sodas aren't bad, either!"

Matt laughed. "How about these ice-cream cones dripping all over the place?"

"Melted plastic and glue," Gram confided.

Matt stepped forward for a closer look. His fingertips skimmed the arrowheads and wampum beads that lay buried in the sand beneath a pair of fashionable moccasins. "I see there's some serious stuff mixed with the humor," he said.

Gram gushed: "I like the way Annie pasted rows of wampum beads around the edges, like a frame. Clever girl."

"Very clever," Matt agreed as his eyes traveled along the beads. "She's learned how to read wampum messages."

Annie said, "It's like reading a secret code. And I'm the master spy."

Matt had already turned to the pile of sketches on the dining-room table. "What's all this?"

"My sketches. Gram wanted to see them before I put them away."

"The tourists will eat them for breakfast," Gram said. "They devour anything I put on the table."

"Who could blame them?" Matt teased. "You serve the best food east of the Rockies."

Gram elbowed Matt. "You'll say anything to get a piece of my blueberry pie."

Matt put his arm around Gram's waist. Annie could tell that Gram was crazy about Matt. Again that unsettling feeling took over. She couldn't help but wonder if Matt had worked his way into Gram's heart because he wanted something.

"This group is *Sun Time*," Annie said, nodding toward the sketches in the center of the table. "I'm going to complete a series of oil paintings based on these sketches for my senior project. The chairman of the art department gave his approval."

"You'll be famous someday," Matt said. "You'll be known as the 'Sewanhacky Artist.' " He noticed her inquisitive expression. "*Sewanhacky* is the Montauk word for Long Island."

He looked from one sketch to the next. "They really burst with activity," he said, admiring the whal-

ers, armed with harpoons, who raced to the open seas
in dugouts and the hunters, camouflaged like a leafy
trees, who chased deer with bows and arrows.
"You've shown a very rugged look at Montauk life,"
he commented. "Did you sketch anything to show
their spiritual nature?"

"Yes." Annie sifted through a stack. "I've labeled
these *Moon Time*. They need more work."

"I like them." He held one at arm's length. An
entire Indian family was gathered at day's end to eat
and tell stories. The elders offered whale fins and
tails to the Great Spirit. One couple, looking into the
glowing embers, embraced as the children retired to
the warm animal skins layered across the sleeping
platforms. Another couple gazed at a ceremonial
string.

Matt peered intently at the sketch. "You haven't
filled in the design on the ceremonial string," he said.

"I haven't decided on the message."

Gram blurted out, "You should see all the wampum designs she photocopied. Her room is bursting
with them."

"I'd like to see them," Matt said. "How about right
now?"

Annie said, "Maybe another time. They're not very
organized."

He gathered her sketches and stacked them in an
orderly pile. "I'd really like to see them." His voice
was insistent.

"Okay, I'll get them," Annie said. She was at her
bedroom door when the thought crossed her mind.

He's a Revington; he always gets his way. She returned to the dining room with the photocopies, still wondering what Matt was so eager to see.

"Thanks," Matt said, taking the photocopies. He quickly worked his way through the ceremonial strings. He studied the wampum belts, pausing to hold up some to the light.

"You seem disappointed," Annie said when he'd finished. "What did you expect to find?"

"I'm not sure." He ran his fingers through his hair. "I thought maybe . . ." His voice, heavy with sadness, trailed away.

She said, "If it's about the wampum designs, I already told you several times on the telephone that none of them reminded me of the Shells. And none of the research I ran across mentioned the Shells." A wall of mystery surrounded Matt, one that Annie wanted to knock down. But something held her back. The same feeling came over her when she read a novel. She wanted to know the ending. But she always put off reading the final few pages. When she could no longer stand the suspense, she would finish the book. A feeling of disappointment would immediately overwhelm her, followed by a sense of loss, as if she'd misplaced a treasured possession.

"I'm going to bed," Gram said. "Lock up for me, Annie. And Matt, don't forget we have to finish our gin-rummy game sometime soon." She disappeared up the back stairs toward the private quarters she and Annie shared.

"I missed you, Annie." Matt's blue eyes glistened

under the fluorescent lights. "I've thought about you a lot. I've been looking forward to seeing you every day." He took Annie's hand and laced his fingers through hers. He leaned over to kiss her.

Instinctively, Annie turned her head to the side. "Matt, can't we just be friends?"

"I'd like to be more than friends," he replied. He stood up and drew Annie to him.

Annie stepped away. Her back pressed into the doorframe. Matt circled her in his arms. He felt so solid and strong.

Annie felt his breath, his arms tightening around her, the warmth radiating from his chest. She wanted him to hold her and kiss her. She wanted that more than anything in the world. She felt herself melting in his arms. He held her tight, and she found it difficult to resist the compelling heat of his body. He tilted his head to kiss her. She turned away. His lips caught the side of her mouth. The kiss was sweet, tentative. She opened her mouth to speak. Their lips came together. Something exploded deep inside Annie. "Please, Matt, don't," she said.

Matt backed away slightly. He cupped her face in his hands. "You and your sketches cast a spell over me," he said. He ran his knuckles lightly down her cheek, then placed his hands on her shoulders and kissed her on the forehead. Without another word, he turned and left.

Annie leaned against the doorframe. Her breath caught in her throat. *Get hold of yourself, Annie. He's money. He's a racer. Don't let this happen. And don't forget, he has a roving eye.*

Annie climbed the stairs and tiptoed past Gram's room.

"Annie," Gram called softly, "you like Matt, don't you?"

"We have nothing in common, Gram."

"You have a lot in common. You're both surviving in this world without parents. Yours are gone. His never made time for him. Annie, the poor don't have a monopoly on loneliness."

Annie took a few steps.

Gram's voice followed her down the hallway. "A guy like Matt Revington comes along once in a lifetime."

Annie fell into bed. She was exhausted, but she couldn't sleep. Her mind raced. She couldn't shed the feeling that she was being set up by Matthew Revington. But set up for what? And the way he searched through her sketches and photocopies. He was up to something. Things were not as they seemed.

Chapter Five

Annie drummed her fingers nervously on her clipboard while Matt drove the marina truck through the early-morning Grayrocks streets. "Are you sure we have everything we need?" She scanned the food chests, tents, camping gear, and cartons brimming with art supplies and cameras.

"Yes, ma'am," Matt said. He swung past the Corner Cafe and approached the marina. "You went over every detail with me a hundred times on the phone this past week. Relax. We'll do just fine."

His confidence soothed her. The stress that had built up from final exams, art projects, and the expedition preparations began to disappear. She sat back and enjoyed the sun peeking through the morning mists. "It's going to be a beautiful day," she said, and tossed the clipboard onto the dash.

"The first of many beautiful days together," Matt said.

At the traffic light, he leaned over the steering wheel and peered through the windshield. "Nothing rivals the beauty of the sun rising over water." He turned and looked into Annie's eyes. "Out west, everyone admires the setting sun. It always made me lonely."

"So you came back east to watch the sun shine on Grayrocks Bay," Annie teased.

"No," he said. "I got tired of all that loneliness."

In spite of herself, Anne knew she was falling in love with Matt. He was the most handsome man she had ever known. She couldn't stop looking at him. His deep tan accentuated his slim but muscular arms and legs, his high cheekbones, and the bridge of his nose. She realized that his blue eyes would have to be reckoned with every day she spent with him. Maybe Gram was right. The Matt Revingtons of this world come along only once in a lifetime.

"We look like partners," Annie said. They both wore the Grayrocks summer uniform of sneakers, cutoff jeans, and navy T-shirts. Any similarity she and Matt had, no matter how slight, delighted Annie.

"We *are* partners," he said emphatically.

Matt drove into the marina's parking lot. The crunching of oyster shells beneath their tires was the only noise they heard as they passed the machine shops and bait shanties. Matt turned in front of the business offices. They were perched on pilings and jutted out over the water like hungry birds. He continued beyond the sign that said AUTHORIZED PER-SONNEL ONLY and parked near the boathouses. A private boat slip boasting the name REVINGTON harbored a sleek beauty that slept eight.

"There she is," Matt said. "My uncle's charter boat. Our home away from home." The name *Island Hoppers* arched majestically across the stern. A sense of adventure swept over Annie. She couldn't wait for the expedition to begin. She looked forward to seeing the islands with a new appreciation for the Montauk culture.

Side by side, Annie and Matt worked quickly, comfortable around each other, like old and trusted friends. But when Annie went belowdecks and opened the door to the storage area, she was surprised. "How did all this lighting equipment and cave gear get here?" she asked.

Matt replied, "I loaded stuff on board last night when the marina was empty. I don't want to call attention to our project."

Annie sensed Matt's nervousness. Was he being completely honest with her? Why this secrecy? She heard footsteps.

A tall, good-looking man dressed in white approached. To Annie, he epitomized the weekend sailor who enjoyed being called "Captain" by tourists who couldn't tell a clam from an oyster.

Matt said, "Annie, I'd like you to meet my uncle, David Revington."

"Pleased to make your acquaintance," he said.

Annie recognized him from pictures she had seen

in the *Grayrocks Gazette* and from those rare occasions when he appeared in town to transact business at the bank. He hardly ever came to his marina. According to the Corner Cafe crowd, he didn't like to leave the bar stools or golf carts at the East Bay Country Club to dirty his hands with fish oil and boat grease.

Matt and his uncle shared the same striking good looks. But whereas Matt personified casualness, David exuded elegance. David possessed a certain wariness, encouraged by locals who delighted in snubbing him or setting him up for one embarrassment or another.

"Pleased to meet you," Annie said. She was torn between being friendly for Matt's sake or aloof in keeping with Grayrocks's traditions. An awkward silence followed her words. Sensing that Matt and his uncle wanted to speak privately, she added, "Excuse me. I'll stow my gear in the cabin."

"First one on the left," Matt called over his shoulder.

From belowdecks, Annie heard the uncle's muffled voice. "Very pretty, but remember your father's warning. Don't get mixed up with a town girl."

Annie was too upset to listen to another word. Fuming, she slammed doors and drawers as she jammed clothes into the bureau. She knew her cheeks were burning. Town girl! Is that what Matt thought of her?

To cool her fire, Annie yanked open the porthole window. She heard Matt and Uncle David say good-bye. Silence followed, then other voices. She leaned forward, shut her eyes, and let the dewy air bathe her face. Hearing a whispered exchange, she stepped closer to the porthole.

"Dr. Winfield, we need to talk."

"Did you experience any trouble with the locals, Matt?"

"No."

"Outsiders?"

"No."

"Does Annie suspect anything?"

"No, Dr. Winfield. She's not the suspicious type."

What was going on here? Annie wondered. What had she gotten herself into? She could get out of this right now. And do what? Work in the cannery? No, thanks! She would take her chances. Maybe she had misunderstood. They *were* whispering.

Slowly and carefully, Annie closed the porthole. Methodically, she stashed her art and photography supplies in cabinets over the bunk bed. In an effort to gain control of herself, she placed her cosmetics in the medicine cabinet one by one, systematically lining up the labels.

"Hey, Annie," Matt called. "Dr. Winfield and the others have arrived. Come on up and meet everybody."

Annie hurried up the steps, determined to forget what she had heard. Or thought she'd heard.

Topside, a stocky, white-haired man in khaki shorts and shirt and a safari hat pumped Annie's hand exuberantly. "You must be Annie," he said. "I'm Dr.

Winfield, and these hearty souls, George and Ginny, are my graduate students from Andrews University."

A man and woman, slathered in white suntan lotion and wearing visors, sunglasses, and noseguards, although the sun had barely risen, stepped forward to meet Annie. Their handshakes were firm, their smiles warm and generous. To Annie, they looked like the typical Grayrocks tourists. Having spent most of their lives indoors, they faced Mother Nature as if war had been declared.

"George and Ginny and I constitute what I affectionately call the A-Team," Dr. Winfield said. Moving between his students, he pulled them close to him with his huge pawlike hands. His gruff voice couldn't conceal his pride in George and Ginny. "This expedition and the research they will gather is part of their master's degree studies. I'm sure the research will find a place in the thesis that each will write. I'm here not as their mentor but more like Big Brother, making sure their findings are accurate."

Dr. Winfield's brows arched above the rims of his thick glasses. "Monetary renewals from the Andrews University grant committee and the reputation of the program—all that good stuff lies in the balance." He patted George and Ginny affectionately. "Matt's only known George and Ginny a few months, but he'll back me up. They're top-notch."

"Sorry to interrupt," Matt said from the bridge. "We're ready to cast off. It's an hour trip to the Shells, in rough waters."

The engine sputtered, then roared. *Island Hoppers* headed away from the marina.

"The waters ahead in Widow's Cove are treacherous," Annie warned. "The surge and storm tides keep things roiled up. It's best to put on your life preservers and stay seated."

She leaned into the wind. "Old-timers believe the ghosts of the Montauk Indians spook these waters to stop tourists from overharvesting the clams and oysters." The appreciative smiles of the A-team told Annie that they enjoyed local lore.

As Matt guided *Island Hoppers* through the rough chop, Annie answered the A-Team's questions about the area. She tried to point out the Old Stone Church steeple, the cupola on the roof of the new library, the observatory telescope on Indian Mound Monument, and other Grayrocks landmarks, but the A-Team constantly interrupted. They wanted to know about the locals. How many might come to the Shells? How often did they go there? Could their approach be detected from everywhere on the island? *Such picky questions*, Annie thought. They were missing the beauty and charm of her hometown and its surroundings.

Reaching calmer waters, Matt followed the channel buoys. Passing beyond the stone breakers, he entered the great V, the open waters between Long Island's north and south forks.

Annie was intent on calling attention to the area she loved. "We'll be passing Gardiner's Island, then Plum Island," she said. "They were dumped here by the same glaciers that laid down the slit for Gray-rocks's potato farmers."

She gripped the railing as the wind picked up. *Island Hoppers* dipped and rocked. "You can always count on riptides and turbulence here," she hollered over the pounding surf and whipping wind.

George and Ginny had turned as green as frogs.

Dr. Winfield hung his head over the side of the boat. "I wasn't expecting a typhoon," he lamented.

"Landlubbers," Annie muttered, and shook her head. Trying to get their minds off the pitching seas, she said, "As you probably know, the Montauks called Gardiner's Island 'Manchonake,' the Island of the Dead."

"Yes," George moaned, "and now I know why. Just leave me here. Retrieve my bones on the return trip."

Ignoring him, Annie continued: "Well, here's a romantic tidbit. The great Montauk sachem Wyandanch—*sachem* was their word for 'chief'—gave the island to his friend, Mr. Gardiner. It was a reward for negotiating the safe return of his daughter, Heather Flower. She'd been captured by a marauding tribe during her wedding ceremony. Ever since, the seaworthy men Grayrocks have courted their women here. They believe romance, not death, rules these waves."

Ginny raised her head. "Hey, Matt, who have you been bringing here?"

High waves smacked the boat. Sheets of water

bombarded the starboard side, soaking Ginny, George, and Dr. Winfield.

Annie tossed them towels. "We're approaching Plum Island. We call these rip currents 'Wyandanch's Revenge.' "

Ginny lurched forward. "Worse than at Gardiner's Island?" she asked feebly.

"Afraid so," Annie said. "Apparently, Wyandanch regretted selling Plum Island for one measly coat, a barrel of biscuits, and a hundred fishhooks."

Matt steered *Island Hoppers* through the hammering waves as the ebbing tide fought the northwest blow off the stern. Wrestling with the wheel, he veered due east toward the Shells. They lay at the gateway to the Atlantic. Their only protection from the powerful ocean currents and treacherous surf were the craggy shores of Montauk Point to the south and Orient Point to the north.

"The worst is over," Annie said. She breathed more easily.

Annie had felt nervous all week. She realized that her summer salary might rest on the success of this first weekend. She needed every dollar she could earn for her senior year. Art and photography supplies as well as résumé and portfolio costs and interviewing trips would devour her meager budget. She didn't know how she would get along with the group. That had made her even more nervous.

The A-Team, however, turned out to be likable people, and Annie's fears soon disappeared. As they talked about their research and their anticipated digs on the Shell Islands, Annie sensed that they were dedicated archaeologists enjoying a break from libraries and laboratories.

Annie studied them. George and Ginny, about the same height and weight, had the lean, muscular bodies of cave climbers. George, in his early twenties, blond, with a quizzical look on his face, constantly struggled to find his sea legs while attempting to transcribe into his journal everything he saw and heard. Annie surmised that Ginny, an attractive redhead with freckles, was slightly older, maybe twenty-four.

Everything about Ginny signaled quickness. She moved fast. Her fingers flew in all directions. She talked in rapid spurts, stopping at the last possible second to catch her breath. She nodded her head when others spoke as if once the sentence was begun, she knew where it would end.

Ginny frequently touched George's arm or shoulder in an aggressive way. There was something almost predatory about her actions. Annie wondered if Ginny wanted to show her that George was taken. Were Ginny and George involved?

"Annie," Ginny said, "I'm not feeling well. Would you come below deck with me?"

"Sure," Annie said. "I'll get you some motion pills."

Once inside Annie's cabin, Ginny spun around, her face close to Annie's. "We need to get something straight. I can tell Matt's interested in you. It's written all over his gorgeous face every time he looks at you. Either you're playing hard to get or you're not interested. Well, I am. I'm looking for some fun when we land on this island, and Matt's perfect. I'll do anything to have him. And I mean anything. So keep your distance. I don't intend to be alone. Do I make myself clear?"

Bowled over by Ginny's blunt attack, Annie mumbled, "Perfectly clear." She turned and hurried out the door. *Watch your back,* she told herself, taking the steps two at a time.

Chapter Six

"**B**ig Shell Island, coming up," Matt announced. "Ten miles by eight of uninhabited terrain." Dr. Winfield, George, and Ginny scanned the open waters. Heavy morning fog shrouded the shoreline and limited their view. "You'll see magic any minute now," Matt said as he slowed the engine.

George's eyes grew round with wonder. "Look at the size of those cliffs," he said, admiring the jagged wall that rose abruptly two hundred feet above the beach. "I see why the Montauks loved this island. Montauk means fortified place."

"That's one interpretation," Ginny said. "Personally, I like 'men of steel.' The French *méteaux,* the steel drill used in wampum making, plus *hock,* and Algonquin word meaning men of."

"You're just plain man-crazy," George teased. He

ducked but was too late. Ginny grabbed him around the neck and kissed him on the cheek.

"Montauk also means uncertain," Matt said.

Annie thought she caught an exchange of knowing glances between Matt and Dr. Winfield. Was it her imagination? Did the Montauk name hold special meaning to them?

"Hold tight, everybody," Matt said. "We'll hit some strong winds as we swing around to the other side of the island."

Matt steered *Island Hoppers* past the stubs of pilings from decayed jetties. He pulled alongside the only usable dock on the island, and Annie jumped off to secure the ropes. Gulls, picking at the shoreline, turned their heads and stared for a moment, then continued their food search.

Ginny was awestruck. "White sandy beaches. Towering trees. This is paradise." She tugged down her visor and gazed to the east at the hollows and rolling hillocks. Turning to the west, she saw fields meandering down to the beach and, in the distance, slopes covered with gnarly trees and wind-trimmed shrubs.

Annie struggled with the ropes. "You're in for some tough terrain. Big Shell's more rugged than the flat coastal plains of mainland Long Island."

"Now come on, little Annie girl, you can't deny the solitude and natural beauty of this place," Ginny said.

"Enjoy it while you can." Annie was annoyed that Ginny spoke to her in such a condescending way.

"By law, the Shell Islands will remain part of the state park system for only another few months. After that, they're up for grabs. My grandmother's the president of S.O.S., the Save Our Shells Committee. She predicts a bitter fight between the environmentalists and the land developers. She's organized a letter-writing campaign to stir up our representatives in Washington."

Dr. Winfield snapped his fingers. "Patience isn't always a virtue. George and Ginny, come with me. We'll gather samples immediately."

"Go ahead," Matt said. "Annie and I will set up camp on the beach."

"They're like kids on a holiday," Annie said. She watched them, distant figures shimmering in the sunlight. Ginny scrambled up a grassy bluff. Dr. Winfield, hunched over the tide line, gathered shells. George sprinted down the beach toward the cliffs.

By noon, Matt and Annie had pitched the tents and unloaded the gear. "Mmmm, Grayrocks chowder," Matt said as Annie swirled a ladle through the kettle hanging over the smoldering fire. "What makes it so delicious?"

"If you asked the cafe regulars, they'd tell you the distinctive flavor comes from a spoonful of experience, a cup of suspicion, a quart of old wives' tales, and a gallon of local wisdom."

"Reminds me of the day we met." Matt knelt beside Annie. He put his hand over hers and helped stir the chowder. "I hope you'll go easier on the pepper than Sally did."

The excited voices of the A-Team interrupted their laughter. Dr. Winfield, George, and Ginny struggled toward camp, all talking at once, their happy faces beaded with perspiration. They set down their bulging backpacks and collapsed on the white sand.

"Show-and-tell time," Dr. Winfield said, wiping his brow. "You begin, Ginny."

Ginny spread plastic pouches from her backpack on a blanket. "Have you ever seen such rich soil?" She wiggled a packet of red clunky clay. "And look." She held up a graph map of the island and a notebook. "Pages and pages already filled with notations."

Annie set out tuna salad on rolls and bowls of clam chowder. A curious look crossed her face. Unwrapping Gram's blueberry pie, she asked, "What do these soil samples have to do with your master's thesis and this expedition?"

Ginny held out her cup, and Dr. Winfield filled it with iced tea. Her hand trembled. Why was she so nervous? Annie wondered. "An analysis of soil samples will support my thesis, 'The Disintegration of the Montauks.' The percentage of soil nutrients and shell fragments at various levels will show that the Montauks found little time for planting when forced to endure the hardships of shell enslavement. As for this expedition..." Ginny took several quick breaths, and her nostrils flared over her full lips. "I'm the chemical expert. Any traces of shells in the soil samples will tell me we're on the right trail leading to where there might be more. We hope to find the center of the Montauks' settlement."

"It's like you're playing detective," Annie said.

Ginny rolled her eyes. "An oversimplification," she said condescendingly.

Dr. Winfield put down his sandwich and smiled at Ginny. "Ginny's too modest to tell you that she's a highly qualified specialist in the chemical properties of shells. She's aware of how certain shells stand up to the elements. Wait till you see her work wonders with a sifting device. A speck of residue, detected by our eagle-eye Ginny, will lead us to the center of the Montauk world. As we speak, the laboratory technicians at Andrews University await our samples. If Ginny should miss anything, and I doubt that will happen, they'll spot it."

Dr. Winfield isn't only Ginny's mentor, Annie decided. *He's her number-one fan and protector.*

Dr. Winfield turned toward George. "Equal time for you, George. Care to enlighten Annie about your work?"

George slurped down his chowder and wiped his mouth. "I'm betting the shells weakened over the years, causing the decline of the wampum business." His facial muscles twitched. Annie wondered if Ginny's nervousness was catching.

"My thesis is called 'The Role of Wampum in Diplomacy,'" George said. "In a nutshell, wampum validated alliances and solidified treaty proposals." He tilted his head back and drained his iced tea. "It's a lively topic because the Montauks loved theatrics. Whooping it up, they reacted to a proposal by shaking the wampum belt in the air or throwing it on the ground. If angered, they kicked the belts away or threw them in the face of the messenger."

Matt said, "Sounds like the reception the cafe regulars give a newcomer."

Annie laughed.

"Even when written treaties were drawn up between whites and Indians," George continued, "the Montauks insisted on wampum messages. They had seen the white man's trickery with a compass, pen, and ink. But they also found the wampum to be more expressive." He tossed the remainder of his roll to the line of gulls that watched from the sidelines. "I'd give anything to come up with even one string of wampum. I can't imagine the thrill of being the first person to interpret the design."

George reached forward and quickly sliced the blueberry pie into six equal pieces. He passed out plates loaded with the plump berries and flaky crust.

Annie shook her head. "Finding a buried wampum string or wampum belt? That's twenty-million-to-one odds, like winning the lottery."

George scooped the extra slice of pie onto his plate. "Eat up," he said, swirling his fork in the air over his double helping.

Annie persisted. "What made you think you'd find a cache of wampum on these islands? Certainly the Montauks would have taken their wampum with them."

Annie looked from George to Ginny to Dr. Winfield and finally to Matt. They avoided eye contact. Annie felt a chill wriggle up her spine. "There's something you're not telling me," she said, jumping up. "What's going on? Why are you really here?"

Ginny bolted to her feet. "You little fool, we're looking for a buried treasure. We need you in case the locals get nosy. Your job is to get rid of them for us."

"Is this true?" Annie asked Matt. Tears stung her eyes.

"It's not like that," Matt said, coming to her side. "Ginny's just trying to make trouble." He glared at Ginny.

George patted Annie's arm. "Ginny's jealous of you. Don't take it personally. She sharpens her claws on everyone who wears a skirt. We put up with her because she's our best climber."

Dr. Winfield stepped between Ginny and Annie. "And without equal when it comes to the safety of our equipment. But she's keyed up and spoke without thinking." He narrowed his eyes. "Isn't that right, Ginny?"

Ginny's lips turned to a hard, straight line. "Maybe I overstated things a bit," she said.

"Go easy from now on, Ginny," George scolded. "We don't want your lies and nastiness to jeopardize the expedition." He spat his words. "You're as acid as your chemical tests. I'd take bets on that."

Annie faced Matt. "I should have known better than to listen to a Revington."

Matt backed away, his hands in the air as if he were being held up at gunpoint.

Dr. Winfield rose to his full height. "That's enough!" he boomed. "Keep on like this and bitterness and hatred will destroy us. Let's start acting like the civilized creatures we pretend to be." He turned toward Annie. "I apologize for not telling you everything and for not letting the others tell you, either. But I have good reason. Walk with me down the beach and I'll explain."

"This better be good," Annie muttered. She had never felt so vulnerable. She had no way off the island except on Matt's boat, and she knew little about the A-Team. Dr. Winfield's fierce loyalty toward Ginny and George included a boatload of arrogance. She didn't know whom to trust.

Dr. Winfield steered Annie toward the cliffs. Away from the others, he stopped and fixed his hard, shining eyes on her. "I won't let friction between you and a team member hinder this expedition. Our work here is much more important than you realize."

Annie crossed her arms over her chest. "So important that you kept me in the dark," she said crossly.

Dr. Winfield continued: "Recently the Andrews University computer and I picked up some privileged information from Wisconsin. It was relayed between members of Madison University's archaeology department. I'm working strictly on a need-to-know basis, but I can tell you this. Those Wisconsinites are on to something big. They've got documentation that an important treasure lies buried here. It's something that could affect the future of the Shell Islands." He kicked a stone and watched it skitter along the sand. "I'm not prepared to say anymore now. And for reasons I can't explain at the moment, I won't allow this matter to be discussed except in my presence. Is that understood?"

Too stunned to object, Annie nodded.

"George and Ginny and Matt have known about this for several months. They've already agreed to my demands. I need that same commitment from you."

Annie didn't know what to say. This might explain the whispered conversation she'd overheard on the boat. It could also explain Ginny and George's nervousness when they discussed the soil samples. Gazing at the pristine beach and its natural vegetation, Annie breathed in the salty air. Images flashed through her mind. She saw her mother, father, and grandmother hard at work preparing posters, making telephone calls, and instigating letter-writing campaigns to save the Shell Islands.

Dr. Winfield interrupted Annie's thoughts. "I couldn't tell you about the treasure before. Small-town grapevines move faster than summer lightning."

Annie looked again at the beautiful beach. She knew what her parents and grandparents would say. "I'll go along with your decision, Dr. Winfield. I don't understand it completely, but I promise not to ask any questions about the treasure. I'll help with the research . . . and the search."

When Annie and Dr. Winfield returned to the group, he proudly announced, "She's one of us."

Matt's smile convinced Annie that she had made the right decision. George and Ginny smiled their appreciation too. A full round of apologies led to promises of complete honesty.

But there it was again. That locking of eyes. That look of conspiracy between Matt and Dr. Winfield. What were they up to? And why were they leaving out George and Ginny? And her?

Dr. Winfield shook Annie's hand. "I knew you were the right person for this job. In fact, I propose a toast." He stood and raised his glass of iced tea. "Here's to Annie Devane, a superb addition to our expedition."

George, Ginny, and Matt rose and clinked glasses. "To Annie," they toasted.

"To us," Annie replied. She wondered if all archaeologists were as temperamental as the A-Team.

Dr. Winfield said, "This afternoon we'll collect samples. Tomorrow we'll hunt for treasure in Hidden Cave. We need to work fast. The Madison archaeology department plans to present their information in the September issue of their journal. That'll call out every treasure hunter in the country, and our opportunity will be lost forever. I've invited Donald Eagleton to help us."

Matt moved close to Annie. "Donald Eagleton's daughter, Aurora, a member of the Shinnecock tribe, is married to Dr. Winfield. Donald's the keeper of the pipe."

Chapter Seven

"**D**elicious lunch," Dr. Winfield said as he shook the sand from his clothes. "Ginny, George," he said, snapping his wrist like a lion tamer cracking a whip, "you'll come with me to gather soil and shell samples. Annie, stay here and process the finds as we bring them back. And Matt, I'll count on you to prepare us for an afternoon dive. Set up scuba equipment and check the air tanks. Okay, everybody. Let's hop to it."

Dr. Winfield sprinted across the sand. Ginny and George grabbed their gear and took off after him.

The sun beat down, and the temperature rose into the nineties. Annie spread a blanket in the shade of the dock and fanned out her laptop computer, camera, sketch pads, and research books. She skimmed the material in *Shells and Soils,* then opened *Indian Leg-*

ends. The introductory words hit her. "Wampum means nothing to the white man. It is everything to the Indian. The tree of our land touches the heavens. Beneath the great tree lies the wampum, whose bearer binds all nations."

Could a wampum belt be buried here? Annie wondered. *Was that the hidden treasure?* Annie wanted to discuss this with Matt. Then she remembered her promise to Dr. Winfield not to talk about the treasure unless he was present. *Hey, wait a minute!* Dr. Winfield had separated her from the group when he'd offered an explanation. Maybe he'd told a different story to Matt, George, and Ginny. Had Dr. Winfield really intercepted a computer message from Madison University? It was all so confusing.

Clattering sounds coming from the dock caught Annie's attention. She looked up and saw Matt. Her eyes hidden behind sunglasses, she watched him unload the scuba masks, fins, and tanks. She regretted lashing out at him. George and Dr. Winfield had vehemently denied Ginny's cruel words that she, Annie, had been hired to fend off nosy locals.

Annie picked up her pad and pencil and began to sketch. With several swift strokes, she captured Matt's long, lean body. Clad in shorts, he glistened in the afternoon sun as perspiration and the spray from salt water ran down his muscular body. His firm biceps flexed. His back and his leg muscles rippled against the weight of the scuba tanks that he lifted from the boat and hauled to the dock. Annie took great pains to capture the strength of each muscle.

His countenance was a mixture of determination, annoyance, and joy. But determination prevailed as she sketched creases across his forehead. Hardest to portray was the character in his haunted, piercing eyes. They were even more penetrating than she had realized. She traced the shape of his lips. Remembering their warmth, she couldn't stop herself from dreaming dreams and longing for more of Matt's kisses.

Returning to her sketch pad, she drew Matt's profile, defining the angles of his prominent nose and strong jaw. She crumbled the sketch. Too harsh. The elusiveness of his gentler side defied the bold black lines.

Annie began again and captured Matt on a beach swept clean by the wind. He was tossing bait fish to seagulls circling in the cloud-stacked sky. *Much better,* she told herself, *but still not right. More imagination, that would do it.* She sketched again, placing Matt in a birch canoe. He paddled past the cliffs, beyond the clam beds and oyster harbors, toward the churning waves. His long hair blowing in the wind, he exuded an untamed quality. *Matt's a Montauk,* she thought, *free and independent, in harmony with his world.*

Matt stopped working and looked at Annie. "A penny for your thoughts," he said.

"Tell me about Donald Eagleton." Annie flipped the sketches of Matt to the back of the pad.

Matt lowered himself from the dock to Annie's blanket. "Donald's a very complex man. He's hard to describe in a few words. What do you want to know?"

"For starters, his beliefs."

Matt grabbed a towel and began to dry himself. "He believes that the powerful spirit of Quashawan, who ruled her people in the 1660's, still protects the Shell Islands. He believes she'll help us find what we're looking for."

Annie rolled her eyes. "I'm sorry, Matt, but I don't see how the spirit of a chief who's been dead for hundreds of years can help us find anything."

"Keep an open mind, Annie. That's all I ask. Tonight Donald will lead us in a ritual drama. He'll accompany his pipe smoking with songs, chants, and stories to awaken Quashawan's spirit."

"It all sounds weird to me."

"You'll change your mind once you've met Donald. He's a modern man who holds on to the old ways of his people."

Annie shrugged her shoulders. "Will anything be expected of me at this, what did you call it, ritual drama?"

"Nothing. But you can participate if you want to. The rest of us plan to encourage Donald. He, in turn, will inspire us. We hope something that's said or done will reveal an important location that we might overlook."

The rest of us? We? The words stung. Annie felt left out. Now she, not Matt, was the outsider, and she didn't like the feeling at all.

* * *

Ginny, George, and Dr. Winfield climbed down from the bluffs and approached the dock.

"These finds should keep Annie busy for a while," Ginny said, unloading her backpack at Annie's feet. A forced smile crept across her face.

"Hot work out there," George complained as he knelt down and added his finds to the pile. Brushing past Annie, he whispered, "It's always hot when Ginny's around. Just ask Matt. He took her out a few times."

Annie returned George's smile with a nasty look.

"Come on, George," Ginny said. "Let's head over to the boat and change into our bathing suits."

"You too," Ginny said, grabbing Matt around the waist. "Three's not a crowd in my book."

As *Island Hoppers* roared away toward a sandbar, Annie spread out the plastic bags. They were filled with soil and shell samples and slips of paper with notations. She pushed Ginny's samples aside. *She can go last,* Annie told herself.

The first bag Annie opened was George's. It contained a whelk shell, from area C-4. Annie photographed the shell, washed it, dried it, and placed it in a clean plastic bag. She secured the bag with an arrow-shaped label and assigned it the number one. Working methodically, she finished bagging all thirty-five samples. She pulled the computer onto her lap, ready to enter the information. But something nagged at her. She set the computer aside and thumbed aimlessly through the collection of bags and labels.

Odd, she thought, that archaeologists and land developers were both interested in soil samples. Could the A-Team be working for land developers? Were Matt's father and uncle somehow involved in this expedition, hoping to get their hands on this land to develop it? Annie shook her head at her own foolishness. Maybe Gram had made her suspicious of anyone showing interest in the Shell Island, afraid they'd develop them and destroy their beauty. She tried to push such thoughts aside as she busied herself with the reference books.

Annie held up the first shell again and examined it from all angles. She typed into the lap computer: number one, C-4, whelk. The technical information bored her. She didn't care that whelk, from the Anglo-Saxon word *wealcan*, meant to roll or that a whelk had a univalvular, spiral shell. How boring! She would rather record that the Montauk Indians drilled beads from the whelks to create beautiful wampum belts and ceremonial strings.

Taking a quick break, Annie flipped through the pages of *Wampum Designs and New York History*. She inched her magnifying glass across several spectacular ceremonial strings, then moved on to the wampum belts. She stopped at a page marred by coffee stains. Near the stains she saw faint indentations—squiggles, lines, and loops. It was as if someone, bearing down on a pen or pencil, had written a message that left an imprint on the page.

Curious, she rubbed the tip of her charcoal crayon across the area. She blew away the excess charcoal. Words appeared. *"This is best possibility. It could be doctored. Let me know if I should get started."* The handwriting was angular. Not at all like Matt's open and expressive style. Who had written the message? The handwriting didn't look like George's, Ginny's, or Dr. Winfield's, but she wasn't positive. What did the message mean?

Annie glanced in all directions. No one was near. She peered through her magnifying glass at the wampum belt on the coffee-stained page. According to the text, it depicted the governor of New York shaking hands with the Montauks' chief sachem and, in turn, handing each of the other twelve chiefs of the Montauk Confederation a gift from the white man's world. Annie gasped with delight as she identified a hat, a hoe, and a frying pan. She consulted the text for explanations of the more intricate and symbolic designs.

What, if anything, did that wampum belt have to do with the Shell Islands?

Annie looked at her watch. Time was flying. *Get to work!* she reminded herself. She picked up shell number two and typed the information into the computer. She worked her way through the entire collection. Whew! She typed in the last word and looked up. She had been so engrossed in her work that she hadn't heard the boat's motor. Matt was walking from the dock, carrying bags of shells and sand.

She was dying to tell him about the message, but

her instincts held her back. Something was going on. She didn't know what. And she didn't know whom she could trust.

"How's it going?" he asked.

"Everything I'm recording is so technical," she said, closing the computer. "There's nothing about the mystery and beauty of the island that's around us." She sighed.

"Now maybe you can see why I want to be a racer, not an archaeologist." He pushed back his sunglasses, and a concerned expression crossed his face. "Your shoulders are really sunburned. You'll never sleep tonight." He reached into the expedition's supply kit and pulled out a bottle of suntan lotion. Kneeling behind Annie, he began to rub her shoulders and back. She closed her eyes and enjoyed the cool sensation on her hot skin. His hands caressed her back from her neck to the band of her halter top, then below the band, down and around her waist.

Annie felt awkward, but she didn't want him to stop. "According to George's notes," she said, holding up a plastic bag, "this is a quahog clam shell." She leaned over the reference book. "See how technical this book is? It says the word comes from the Atlantic Coast Narragansett tribe, who called it *po-quauhock*. It should say how pretty that shade of purple is, that the Indians made wampum beads from it." She noticed that George's handwriting didn't match the style of the message.

Matt said, "Relax. Forget this scientific stuff for a

few minutes." He leaned across her to get more sun-tan lotion. His bare chest brushed her back.

Annie felt the beating of his heart. "The quahog's Latin name is *Venus mercenaria,*" she said.

"Hmmm," Matt said. "Venus, goddess of love." He kissed her shoulders and the back of her neck. "I felt bad about what Ginny said to you. I hope there's no misunderstanding between us. I wouldn't lie to you." He kissed her hair. His arms circled her waist, and she leaned back into his embrace. She closed her eyes.

The wind riffled the pages of her dictionary. She opened her eyes, and the word *mercenaria* jumped from the page. *Mercenaria,* a hired servant. Her breath caught in her throat. She remembered Matt's uncle calling her a town girl. *Hired servant, town girl, the same thing.* She pulled away form Matt. "You'd better get back to the others," she said coolly.

"Annie," he said, thrown off balance. His blue eyes searched her face. She looked away.

"Women, I'll never understand them," he mut-tered. "Grayrocks woman, definitely one of life's mysteries," he complained as he walked away.

Annie finished processing all the finds. Dr. Win-field and Ginny's handwriting didn't match the style of the message. She didn't know what to make of anything. Unable to concentrate, she looked toward the sandbar. Matt stood knee-deep in water, his hair whipped by the wind, his broad shoulders and narrow waist outlined by the late-afternoon sun.

He lifted his arms and cast a net high above him.

As if in slow motion, the net soared in the air, spun, and unfurled. For one brief moment it hung suspended, then splashed against the surface of the sparkling water. The tense muscles in Matt's back relaxed, his arms came down to his sides, and the net disappeared in the waves. As Annie watched, Matt reeled in the net, brimming with silvery fish that danced in the sun.

Before long, Matt came ashore again. "I have a few minutes before I pick up the A-Team," he said. He saw the sketch pad and turned back the cover. "Good caricature of Dr. Winfield on safari." He laughed. "With that lion's mane of hair and fresh kill at his feet, I can't tell if he's the hunter or the hunted."

He turned the page. "Ginny would have a fit if she saw herself in this gaudy straw hat and flowered shirt. And the way you painted her features, she looks like a frog in tourist's clothing."

He turned the page and laughed again. "George looks like a happy puppy running along the shore, catching sticks tossed by Ginny."

Annie laughed nervously. She reached for the sketch pad. She tried to take it away from Matt before he turned the page again, but she wasn't quick enough.

"Whoa," he said, his breath taken away by the first sketch of himself. "I don't remember flexing so many muscles or working so hard."

Annie held her breath and closed her eyes as Matt flipped the page.

"Seagulls eating out of my hands?" he asked, turning to look at Annie. "You've got a good imagination."

Annie willed the wind to blow the pages from Matt's hands. She wanted to sink beneath the sand and disappear forever.

Slowly, Matt pulled the next page forward. "Wow!" he said, startled by the sketch. "Warrior Matt attempts to conquer raging ocean. You certainly have a romantic touch. Are you trying to tell me something?"

Annie felt herself blush. There was no escaping the obvious. "You have a great face and body," she said. "I'm sure you've heard that before. Probably from half the women in Grayrocks and East Bay."

Chapter Eight

The sky blazed red, then surrendered to deep blue as evening descended on Big Shell Island. Everyone gathered at the campsite.

Dr. Winfield dug a shallow pit, lined it with rocks, and added kindling wood. "Donald Eagleton has a request," he said. "From the moment we light the cooking fire and the campfire, he asks us to prepare for the ceremony by immersing ourselves in the ways of the Montauks. I'll go first."

He gathered up the corn, ready for roasting, the silk removed, the ears rewrapped in their husks. "Corn was their main staple. They pounded it into meal or boiled it to make a thick porridge." He dropped a handful of seaweed into the pit. Hissing noises ripped through the air.

Matt looked up from the hot dogs he was brushing

with barbecue sauce. "Just as I baste these hot dogs, the Montauks basted their game with bear oil and roasted it over open fires. They preferred wild turkey, but they settled for deer, possum . . . or frog." He winked at Annie and smiled. She laughed, enjoying the thought of Ginny Frog sizzling on the spit.

Glad she had done her homework, Annie held up a woven basket. "The Montauk women gathered hemp, rush, and corn husks in summer and wove them into baskets during the long winter months. They painted designs with colorful dyes. Red came from ocher. Brown from walnuts. And green from seaweed scum that collected on rocks. They called the scum frog spit." She caught Ginny's eye and didn't flinch. Ginny looked away when Matt laughed heartily, as if sensing that the joke was on her.

Ginny, who was setting out plates and silverware, picked up a carving knife. Trailing her forefinger along the blade and licking her lips, she glowered at Annie. "The Montauk women were skillful and quick with knives. They could slice meat from bones in seconds." Her eyes glinted. "That's how they kept away intruders and rivals."

George poured iced tea into glasses. "The Montauks made a bitter tea from beach plums and choke-cherry bark. The men probably drank to forget about knife-happy women." He grinned. "Wouldn't you agree, Matt?"

George took a can of bug spray and proceeded to apply it to his arms. "The Montauks coated their bod-

ies with fish oil or animal fat to discourage insects."
He nodded at Ginny. "They had a pest problem too."

"All this talk and that wonderful aroma from the
pit reminds me that I'm starved," Dr. Winfield announced.

Holding up a platter of sizzling hot dogs, Matt
said, "Dinner's ready, so help yourselves."

Dr. Winfield filled his plate. "Shall we sit in a circle around the campfire?"

Annie sat cross-legged, balancing her plate on her
knees. The campfire suddenly sputtered, and she felt
a blast of cool air. The hair on the back of her neck
rose. She turned and saw, standing behind her, a wiz-
ened old man. He wore moccasins, jeans, and a plaid
shirt. Long braids hung to his waist. His belt buckle
was emblazoned with an eagle's head made of white
and purple beads. He held a bundle wrapped in a
blanket.

"How!" he said as he bent his elbow and raised
his hand.

Dr. Winfield stood. "Stop it, Donald."

Donald's face lit up in a wide, toothless grin. The
deep creases in his face almost swallowed his eyes.
"Show a little respect for your elders," he said, em-
bracing Dr. Winfield. "And allow an old man one of
life's greatest pleasures . . . reinforcing stereotypes."

Everyone laughed and shook hands.

Donald screwed up his face and looked at Annie
through squinted eyes. "Me want that white woman's
scalp," he cackled. "Me like her curly brown hair.
Look like beautiful worms wriggling on fishing hook.

Me no want"—he spun around and pointed at Ginny's red hair—"wet carrots."

Donald's eyes softened. He grinned and approached Annie. "Why is it Indians and Tarzan always begin sentences with 'me' instead of 'I'? First the white man ruins our land, then our grammar. What's this world coming to?"

"How did you get here?" Annie asked, still startled by Donald's arrival. "I didn't hear a boat."

"Flew in with the seagulls," Donald said, and flapped his arms.

"So this is the mysterious Donald Eagleton," Annie said. "I expected the keeper of the pipe to be more, uh, solemn."

Donald laughed. "Tom's tying up the boat. He'll be here in a minute. It was his idea to cut the engine, Annie. He wanted me to sneak up and scare you, but you turned around too soon. Either you're psychic or I'm slowing down in my old age."

"That'll be the day," Dr. Winfield said.

"I'll turn eighty this year." Donald leaned toward Annie. "That's nine hundred sixty moons in Indian lingo." He plunked down next to her.

"Shall we get started?" Dr. Winfield asked.

"Not until my chauffeur and I have something to eat," Donald replied.

"Hi, Annie, everybody." Shells crunched beneath Tom's feet as he approached the campfire. His ruddy complexion turned strawberry red in the fire's glow. He sat down across from Annie, next to Matt. "So, Matt, have you dug up any buried treasure? I figured with the help of these bigwig experts, you'd be a millionaire by now." He guffawed. "I have extra shovels in my garage. Say the word and they're yours."

Annie searched Matt's face but found no reaction.

"Did somebody mention food?" Tom wiped his hands on his jeans and helped himself to a hot dog and bun. He turned to Matt. "I see you've given up Texas steak for Long Island wieners. And blonds for—"

"That's enough," Matt said. "Just eat."

Would Tom have said redhead or brunet? Annie wondered. She was angry that Tom had chosen this special moment to bring up Matt's interest in East Bay's bevy of blonds. She remembered his words on the phone at college: "Matt loves short skirts and long hair."

Everyone ate and talked. Then a peacefulness settled over the group. The waves lapped at the shore. The fire crackled as sticks popped and sent up flames.

In hushed silence, Donald pulled back the corners of the woven blanket. He spread it out on the sand.

Carefully, he removed a basket covered by a brown cloth. Annie couldn't take her eyes off his expressive hands as they lifted items from the basket and caressed each one gently. A pipe, a rattle, a drum. An oak branch, an ear of corn, and a shell. From deep in his throat came mysterious sounds, like the cackling of crows, gurgling streams, winds howling in deep caves. All at once, Donald raised his hands and became silent. He picked up the stem and bowl of a clay pipe and fitted them together.

Flames shot up from the campfire. Embers danced in the smoky air. Annie saw Matt's handsome face in the golden glow of the flames. A warm sensation spread through her body.

Donald rested the pipe across his knees. He closed his eyes and lifted his arms. "Tonight, when all the world rests and sleeps, we call upon our Mother Earth and our Father Sky, upon the spirit beings of our ancestors, upon Quashawan, to help us here in the land they cherished. We are all part of them and they of us. We are all part of the Great Mystery, the total of all things that ever were and ever will be, the oneness of all things."

Donald put a pinch of tobacco in the bowl of the pipe. Matt leaned toward the fire and ignited a braid of marsh grasses. He carried the flame to the pipe and lit the tobacco. Swirling smoke rose into the cool night air. A gentle breeze carried the smoke and encircled the group.

Donald continued: "Let the fragrances of tobacco and grass, Mother Earth's gifts, charge our senses." He puffed on the pipe. Circles of smoke rose. Sweet scents filled the air. Annie breathed deeply and felt something stir deep inside her.

While Donald smoked the pipe and prayed, Dr. Winfield slapped the drum with the flat of his hand, and George shook the rattle. Fast and loud, then slow and soft, the drum spoke, and the rattle kept time with the beat.

"Sacred pipe," Donald chanted, "many speak their prayers on you at births, weddings, and funerals. Help us now transcend our everyday lives. Help us come to the other side. Carry our word to the Great Mystery, to the First Cause of all that was and is and ever will be."

Donald paused and looked around the circle. "You must find the treasure that will help good people retain these islands, these last free and independent ancestral lands. Who among you knows what lands I speak of, the lands stol from the tribes of Sewanhacky?"

"I do," Ginny said.

"Then speak," Donald said, "and I will smoke and pray on the pipe."

"Hear the mighty roll call of the Montauk people. The Corchaug and the Manhasset," Ginny began slowly. "The Massapequa and Matinecock. The Merric and Montauk." Her voice grew stronger. Her breath came more quickly. "The Nissequog and Unkechaug. The Nesaquake, the Patchogue. The Secatogue, Setauket, and Shinnecock. Hear the mighty names of their once proud villages: Aquebogue, Ashamomuck, and Cutchogue. Massapequa, Mattituck, and Merric. Montauk and Nesaquake. Patchogue and Rechquaakie. Listen to the names of their mighty leaders: Wyandanch of the Montauk. Nowedonah of the Shinnecock. Poggatacut of the Manhasset. King David Pharaoh and his son Wyandanch Pharaoh, of the Sewanhacky Confederation."

Donald took an ear of corn from his basket and

held it over his head. "Once, before the old ways crumbled, there were cornfields here. Let us rekindle the old ways and stir up buried memories. Let us dance up the corn."

Matt held out his hands to Annie. She came to him. They danced, slowly at first, the palms of their hands together, their eyes fixed on each other. Then they danced faster and faster. Their bodies reached toward the sky, then bent toward the ground, stretching and bending again and again. Turning, whirling, they moved as one. Together, then apart, then together again, Annie and Matt danced around the campfire.

Ginny stood and pulled George to his feet. She danced with George, then Dr. Winfield, then Tom. She writhed back and forth. Her body glistened. Her hair swung down her back. Her bare feet kicked up sand.

When Annie saw Ginny approaching, she buried her head in Matt's chest and held him tightly. With arms entwined, their legs touching, Annie and Matt embraced. They danced so close that Annie could hardly breathe. They pulled apart as Donald's chanting ceased. Dizzy, her eyes retreating behind her long lashes, Annie lowered her head and tried to catch her breath. She felt very warm, exhilarated from the crackling fire and the sensual dance.

Donald chanted again and ran his hands across the shell and branch from his basket. His voice grew softer. The notes drifted away on the breeze as he wove together the myths of his people. Annie's mind swam with the mysterious images.

Donald said, "Let the spirit of Quashawan direct tomorrow's search."

Annie felt as if she had awakened from a dream. She looked at each person in the glow of the firelight. Everyone appeared transported, touched by Donald's words. Their faces bore a sweetness, a childlike innocence. Even Ginny's. Their expressions conveyed awe of the world around them, wonder at the feelings and thoughts arising within them. The ceremony moved Annie deeply.

Donald threw a handful of sand on the fire. Smoke filled the air. "I feel the presence of Princess Quashawan. Her spirit comes to us in the corn, the branch, the shell, in all these things. She speaks to me of birds. 'Follow the path of birds,' she says." Donald lifted his arms in front of him, palms facing toward the sky. "She's here now, among us."

Donald shook the embers from his pipe. He dipped the bowl of the pipe into a cup of water and wrapped the pipe in his blanket. He crouched before the fire, his dark eyes reflecting the fire's sparks. "The spirit of Quashawan is strong. Hear me! A woman will help you find what you seek. A woman will guide you in preserving this island."

Ginny and Annie looked at each other. Annie didn't know which was stronger, the jealousy or the hostility emanating from Ginny.

"Listen to the waters, flowing and still," Donald said. "Touch the soil where corn once flourished and the sand, where shells abound. Open your eyes to the colors around you and to the circles. The moon, the sun, wigwams, shells, nests, and trees, especially trees, for a flowering tree once filled the center of the earth. Breathe in the earth's fragrances. Savor the four tastes. Do all this and you will find what your heart desires on the fourth day. And now it is over. Go. Sleep. Sleep and dream."

Donald covered the flames with sand. The last thing Annie saw was Matt's face in the glowing light. His eyes, squinted with steely determination, sent a shiver of fear up her spine.

Chapter Nine

"Rise and shine," Dr. Winfield's voice boomed. "Hidden Cave awaits."

Annie pushed aside the flap of her tent. She rubbed her eyes and stared into the early light. The sea air tingled with the aroma of perking coffee and sizzling bacon. Matt knelt over the barbecue pit, humming and shaking the frying pan. Dr. Winfield, George, and Ginny were striding toward the dock. Realizing that she was the last to rise, Annie quickly pulled on her clothes.

"Grab some breakfast, sleepyhead," Matt said. "The others are gathering the climbing gear and lighting equipment. They're going to light up Hidden Cave like a birthday cake." He noticed the dark circles under Annie's eyes. "Hey, are you okay?"

"I'm still groggy. Donald's ritual drama gave me

the strangest dreams. Wampum beads, circles, corn, everything whirled around in my head all night long."

"That's good," Matt said. "The Montauks believed in the power of dreams. Maybe the spirits chose you as their intermediary between the spirit world and the A-Team."

Under Matt's steady gaze, Annie felt she could drown in his deep blue eyes. "Just relax and let the dream messages speak to you," he said.

Annie helped herself to coffee and eggs. "This is my favorite island. I wish we had time to swim and enjoy the view."

"I am enjoying the view," Matt said, looking directly at her.

Annie's cheeks reddened. The morning mists rolled over the scrub grass along the bluffs. "I hope none of this ever changes," she said, struggling to check her desire for Matt.

"Maybe we can preserve this island," Matt said. "The Montauks understood this circle of land and the never-ending circles that shaped their universe."

"There were circles in my dreams," Annie said. "Terrifying circles, like big hoops or holes. Black squawking creatures flew through them, whatever they were." Annie shook her head and looked at Matt with troubled eyes.

Matt set down his fork, forgetting his scrambled eggs. He took Annie's hand and traced the lines of her curved palm with his forefinger. He stretched her hand wide open. "The lines of your hand form the letter M."

"Everybody's hand has an M." She laughed and turned his palm up.

"That's not true," he said. "See these first two lines? They make an A."

"And right next to that A is a C . . . C for cars."

Matt kissed Annie's knuckles. She pulled away and scooped up a forkful of eggs. "We better hurry and clean up," she said. "The troops look about ready, and it'll take us a while to get to the cave."

"Annie," Ginny called from the dock. "Can you help me with this?"

"I'm on my way," Annie said, and sprinted toward her reluctantly.

"Conference time," Ginny said when Annie drew close. "I saw how you held on to Matt when you danced with him last night. Trust me, he'll get tired of your teasing schoolgirl ways. Soon he'll come to me, and I'll be waiting with open arms. He *will* be mine. I've had every man I've ever wanted. Matt's no different. He's just one more challenge. And I love the thrill of the chase. Watch me and you'll see how a real woman gets her man. As I told you before, I'll do anything to have him." Her bold words challenged Annie.

"It's a free country," Annie said. She turned on her heel to leave, then paused for a long moment. "But I don't believe Matt's interested in older women."

"Is Ginny's problem straightened out?" Matt asked when Annie returned.

"Let's say I've got it under control," Annie said.

"Hurry along, everyone," Dr. Winfield urged. He stooped forward with the weight of supplies and equipment. "Now, Annie, where's this Hidden Cave you and most of the folks from Grayrocks have visited?"

He could be down-home nice when he wanted something, Annie decided. "It's at the base of the cliffs. We have to cross the island and approach it from the other side. There's no beach or dock over there, so we have to do this the hard way. It's an-hour-and-a-half trek with all this equipment."

"I love a challenge," Ginny said, and ran her finger under Matt's chin. Annie ignored the exchange.

"Did I hear right that the cave's been abandoned for years?" George asked.

Annie nodded. "Because of its narrow entry, it's too dangerous for tourists. The museums gave up on it too. They wanted to excavate, but the floor's solid rock."

"The museum staff did their best," Dr. Winfield said. "I've seen the bowls, tools, and stone carvings they retrieved."

"Who found the cave, Annie?" George asked.

"Teenagers. During Prohibition, bootleggers hid crates of booze in the cave. There was a flood, and the bootleggers got trapped inside. Their bodies piled up near the entrance when the water receded. Several years later, during a class trip, students from Grayrocks High found the bones. What an uproar! The parents came to Big Shell to see for themselves the mysterious cave. A few crawled inside, but when they saw how dangerous it was, they forbid their children to go there. My mother and father—did I tell you they owned a photography shop in Grayrocks?—they went into the cave. They took photos."

"Before the museum people arrived?" Dr. Winfield asked.

"Yes. The photos are in an album at Gram's. Would you like to see them sometime?"

"We certainly would," Dr. Winfield said. "Bring them back when you pick up supplies this week. In fact, I'd appreciate your making a special trip."

The urgency in Dr. Winfield's voice surprised Annie. What importance could those photos have to him?

Following Annie's lead, Matt and the A-Team trudged uphill. They made their way in an easterly direction along the ridge, passing pine thickets, cranberry bogs, and ponds dotted with ducks. They came at last upon the shadbush tangles of the deer-feed flats. Changing to a northerly course, they circled the swamp and headed toward one of the groves of white birch that proliferated in the shadow of the cliffs. One rugged sweaty hour later, Dr. Winfield suggested they take a break. George and Ginny dropped their equipment and flopped on the ground. Matt and Dr. Winfield meandered over to a maple tree and stretched out in the shade.

Annie started to sit down but changed her mind.

She decided to tell Dr. Winfield that the photos of the cave were faded and probably not very good. As she approached, Matt and Dr. Winfield sat with their backs to her, deep in conversation.

"Do you think back then those bootleggers knew about our treasure?" Dr. Winfield asked.

"I don't know." Matt replied.

Dr. Winfield chuckled. "Come on" he said. "You're a Revington. You're supposed to know about bootleggers."

Annie stopped abruptly. An uneasy feeling settled in the pit of her stomach. Was Dr. Winfield friendly with Matt's family? Was she helping the wrong people take over the Shell Island? She had no proof, only intuition. And her dreams.

Annie quickly retraced her steps.

Refreshed, the group moved on. Annie hitched up her shoulder and shifted the weight of the bundle on her back. As she proceeded toward a clump of cattails hidden in steamy haze, a gaggle of honking geese flew past her. Startled, Annie stepped back. Her foot slipped on a patch of wet moss and sent her flying down the embankment. She reached for a tree branch but missed. She rolled over and over until her knee struck a rock at the bottom of the ravine.

"I'm okay," she called to the faces peering over the rim. Shaken, she lay on the ground looking up at them. Blood trickled down her leg. Matt had already grabbed the first-aid kit and was working his way down to her.

"Easy does it," he said as he helped Annie to a

sitting position. Annie noticed his brow furrowed with concern as he washed her wound with water from his canteen. Gently he applied salve, then bandaged her knee. "That should do for now," he said, tying the gauze securely. He rocked back on his heels to admire his work.

Annie leaned on Matt's shoulder and took a few steps. She felt woozy and weird, as if she had become detached from the scene and saw it as an observer. A picture flashed through her mind of fog swirling around her. She couldn't shake the feeling that she was at the bottom of an embankment, that there had been an automobile accident, that she was in great pain. The picture faded. Her knees buckled, but Matt's strong arms caught her and kept her from falling.

"Nothing's broken," Annie said. She saw relief on the faces of the A-Team. "I don't want to hold up the expedition. Let's keep going."

Annie clenched Matt's callused hands as she climbed the embankment. The men were all so concerned, she must be wrong about them. They couldn't be involved with the land developers. Annie wanted so much to believe, especially in Matt. He was too gently and caring to hurt anyone. But suspicion nagged her like a shell fragment caught in her sandal.

They reached the rocky terrain below the cliffs. Annie stopped. She cocked her ear. "Do you hear that noise?"

"The wind," Ginny said.

"Well, that wind made the legends grow," Annie said.

"What legends?" George asked.

"Unearthly groans of the dead echo through the cave."

A low moan careened through the scrub.

"The cave's ten feet dead ahead," Annie said. She appreciated the A-Team's baffled expressions. Her mother and father's reaction had been similar when they stood in the same spot many years ago, completely unaware that the cave was so close. The bittersweet memory deepened Annie's need to have someone besides Gram to love her, someone to hold her. She might never make it with Matt, she conceded. She had too many doubts. Could she love someone whose family looked down on town girls? Someone who thrived on danger? Someone who might follow in his family's footsteps, making money from stolen land? It could never work. She needed a secure, enduring love.

Annie wove her way through a maze of boulders at the base of the cliff. She ducked beneath the birch branches and stopped before an outcropping of waist-high boulders.

"Hey, that's an unusual rock formation," George remarked. "I'll bet someone set them up like that."

"According to legend," Annie said, "Indian spirits spit these stones from the mouth of the cave to mark the burial site of the bootleggers." She scampered over the stones. "The entrance is over here!"

"There's a more scientific explanation for the formation," Ginny said, oozing superiority. "The repeated thawing and freezing of fissures, those large cracks near the entrance, put pressure on the rock. It shattered, and rock fragments broke away."

"I like the Grayrocks's interpretation better," Matt said.

"I hate to be the bearer of bad news," Ginny said, "but we're looking at talus." She drew in a breath and looked at Annie. "Talus is a pile of rocks that has broken off the cliffs and accumulated here at their base. Talus caves are formed in voids and are usually very small. We won't find much here."

"Trust Ginny to stick to the facts and put a damper on the fun," George said, and stepped past her.

Matt looked up at the cliffs. They towered, dark, mysterious, more foreboding than Annie had remembered. "There could be more here than meets the eye," Matt said to Dr. Winfield.

Three box turtles with spotted shells crept from the shadows into the sunlight. What was Donald's myth about Turtle? This could be a premonition, Annie decided. The treasure might be near.

Ginny was the first to reach the cave's small opening.

"Are you sure I'll fit through there?" Dr. Winfield asked.

"No one's ever gotten stuck before," Annie said.

"Let's hope I'm not the first." He sucked in his breath and patted his flattened stomach.

Annie pointed at the narrow opening. "The museum director said that before the flood and the sand buildup, the Montauks could walk upright through the entrance. He considered blasting, but the cave didn't yield enough treasures. Remember, the opening is low. Be careful."

"Time to get into our gear," Matt said, pulling things from his cave pack. He stepped into coveralls that had leather patches on the upper leg and opposite shoulder, protection against rope burns.

"Let me help," Ginny said. She handed Matt his gloves, rubber knee pads, and hard hat. When she secured a nylon rope around his waist, she hugged him tightly. "A kiss for good luck?" she asked.

"Sure," Matt said. He gave her a reluctant peck on the cheek.

"Let's check supplies," Ginny said.

They all dropped their packs. Ginny inspected the contents, checking off the list as she called out every item from canteen to whistle. She turned abruptly. "Annie, you have your cameras? Good. Take our picture."

Ginny gathered the men around her and struck a flirty pose snuggled against Matt. Containing her jealousy, Annie smiled and snapped several shots.

George clipped a carbide lamp to his helmet. "Let there be light," he said. Helmets and flashlights beamed. He sang off-key: "You light up my life." Everyone groaned, but a cheerful camaraderie settled over the group.

Chapter Ten

Annie took the lead. "If we stagger our departures at three-minute intervals, we won't be on each other's heels. When you enter Hidden Cave, be cautions. Stand up slowly and get your bearings. When your eyes adjust to the dim light, you'll see why the floor is called Dragon's Teeth."

"Dragon's Teeth!" Ginny sniffed. "Is that another quaint Grayrocks label?"

Annie blushed. "There's a rim, actually a ledge about six-feet wide. It encircles the interior of the cave, and you can walk on it. It's a tricky path filled with dragons, uh, sorry, I mean stalactites and stalagmites. So, watch yourself. It's a fifty-foot drop if you misstep."

"Dragon's Teeth." Ginny sneered. "How juvenile. How superstitious. Don't you think so, Matt?"

Three anxious minutes after Annie disappeared into the blackness, Matt crouched on all fours and crawled through the opening on his hands and knees. Hands to mouth, he called, "I'm coming in."

Matt wriggled along the floor, making slow progress in the shifting sugary sand. Annie's muted voice warned, "It's slippery up ahead." No sooner had he heard her han the sandy area ended. A stony, uneven floor, dripping with moisture and coated with a pulpy, spongy mass, swished under his weight

Matt's headlight shined on the craggy surface of the tunnel roof where limestone cracks seeped ribbons of dripstone. White calcite icicles sparkled like fireflies. Matt elbowed his way along the jagged floor, pushing off the sides of the slimy walls with his feet.

"I'm at an arch in the passageway," he called ahead. A few seconds later he added, "The tunnel's much bigger now."

Annie warned, "Be careful not to smack your head or hook your cave pack on a sharp edge."

Matt continued to snake his way forward. "I'm crawling over a small blanket of flowstone," he shouted.

Annie imagined him passing the area where water had seeped down the walls, passed over rocks, and traveled across the floor. It left behind a graceful covering of stone, like a current of rippling water frozen in time.

"The floor's dropping now," Matt said. "I can almost stand."

"Stay low." Annie's voice sounded close. "You'll be out of the tunnel in a minute."

Without thinking, Matt pushed himself upright. He took one step and slipped. "Aagggh!" His arms flailed wildly as he tumbled forward. He careened against one wall, then the other, before falling to his knees.

"What's wrong?" Annie shouted.

Matt fumbled for the rough, uneven wall. "Nothing." He winced as he gripped a jagged edge.

He heard a series of soft clicks. Holding his breath, he turned toward the noise. Two glowing eyes watched from a hole. Seeds, nuts, and bits of tree bark lay scattered nearby. "A rat's keeping me company," he called to Annie.

"Oh? Did Ginny catch up to you?" she asked.

"What's that, Annie? Sounds like the green-eyed monster entered the cave with us," Matt teased.

Annie bit her tongue and affected a laugh.

"The floor's sloping. . . . Now it's leveling off," Matt said. The beam of his headlight shined on Annie's hiking boots, then traveled up her body to her face, which was haloed in the light.

"You can stand up," she said, and helped Matt to his feet. Her voice was amplified by the hard, thick walls. "Don't step on the Dragon's Teeth," she warned, guiding him toward the right. Matt's headlight scanned the round cave, then slowly panned the rim's three hundred sixty degrees. Beautiful, stately stalactites, stalagmites, and columns graced the rim.

They stood like silent sentinels guarding the cave's secrets.

"Let's move aside to give the others room to crawl through," Annie said.

"I'm at the arch." Dr. Winfield's hearty voice echoed through the tunnel. Far, far away Ginny's brash voice called out, "Ready or not, here I come."

Annie and Matt stood in the cool dampness, leaning against the cold rock wall, awed by the majesty and beauty around them. It was as if they were on the edge of two worlds, a universe above them, another below. The beams from their headlight illuminated the cave, one hundred feet from the domed ceiling to the bowllike floor. Reddish brown rock formed the cave walls, glistening with vibrant green and blue hues where water trickled over moss and phosphorescent ore. Eerie shadows created a surreal landscape, alien and remote, like the moon's surface. The formations were mostly white, gray, or cream. Here and there, vivid orange, red, and blue ones glistened like gigantic popsicles.

Matt scanned the wall around the rim with his flashlight. Wet stones shone back. Then the first design appeared, followed by another and then another. "I imagine the Montauks stood on this very spot, creating these designs. What do you make of them, Annie?"

"I see arrows in the lines. Maybe rows of corn over there. Possibly fishing poles. The circles could be wigwams or birds' nests or tree trunks." She laughed. "When we were kids and first saw the cave pictures, we thought the Indians had played tic-tack-toe on the walls. If you look closely, you'll see where kids drew lines around the x's and o's. Sad to say, there's graffiti too."

"Hearts and arrows that say Annie loves Jack or John or Mike?" Matt asked.

Matt and Annie turned toward a noise at the entrance.

Dr. Winfield staggered from the entrance. He slipped, bumped his elbow on the wall, and stumbled. As Matt and Annie tried to help him, his flashlight careened crazily. Kaleidoscopic whirls vibrated around the room. Reds, oranges, greens, and blues danced across the walls.

Dr. Winfield grabbed hold of a jutting wall. He shined his light on a slick and worn area near the entrance. "Aha! There's the culprit! A pack rat's trail. They scurry in and out of caves with their little treasures." He ran his glove along the ledge. "They have lots of company." He examined several cocoons and webs. "Looks like crickets and spiders. Maybe a snake or two."

Annie tugged her collar closely around her neck and shook her legs. Her skin crawled. Hopping up and down, she slapped her sleeves and pants legs.

Ginny arrived next. Her low, breathy voice murmured, "Unbelievable," as her eyes took in the cave's beauty. She stepped into the cave and took several steps toward Dr. Winfield.

A snake slithered down the wall. It wriggled down Ginny's pant leg and disappeared behind her boot.

She let out an earsplitting scream, pushed past Dr. Winfield, and fell into Matt's arms.

Who's she kidding? Annie asked herself. *Helpless female? Ha! Definitely the act of a desperate woman. Well, she said she'd do anything to get Matt.*

Several minutes later, George emerged from the opening. He sucked in air and exhaled noisily. "Ah, cave perfume, my favorite odor. Nothing like a mixture of wet earth, dry dust, and bacteria-infested water to clear the sinuses."

"At least there's no pollen or smog," Ginny added, breathing deeply.

"Cavers, what are we waiting for?" Dr. Winfield asked. "Let's see these delicate ecosystems up close. First, a quick review of our plan so we don't get our signals crossed."

"We start at the base of the cave," George said. "We set up the lights and work our way to the ceiling with our grappling equipment."

Ginny added, "We'll divide the cave in fourths, each taking one section. Annie will photograph every square inch, regular and Polaroid. Let's hope she can keep up with us."

Dr. Winfield added, "We'll try to complete the area below the rim this morning. We'll save above the rim for this afternoon." He stood at attention. "All right, cavers!" he boomed. "On your toes. Remember Donald's advice. Let's use our senses and stay open to all possibilities. This treasure has eluded the casual observer and the museum experts, but we'll find it."

George poked his fingers into several cracks. "We can drop anchor in any one of these."

Dr. Winfield placed a chock, a hexagonal wedge, into a crack and backed toward the edge of the rim. Testing its strength, he pulled the rope taut between the chock and his hands. He grabbed a webbed sling about twelve feet long. Winding it between his legs, behind his backside, across his chest, then over his shoulder and down his back, he fashioned a harness and seat. He hooked both ends of the sling to a descender on his rope. George and Ginny did the same.

"Our turn," Matt said to Annie.

As Annie and Matt completed their harnesses, Dr. Winfield and George backed toward the edge and planted their feet a shoulder's width apart. A cold chill ran up Annie's spine as they stepped backward over the edge. The drills she had practiced with the college spelunkers' club hadn't prepared her for this terror. This was real. She had never actually worked her way over and around a rim.

Annie looked over her shoulder at the edge of the rim. "I'm not sure I can do this," she said.

"Wimp!" Ginny taunted. "This cave's nothing. You should see the big ones like Carlsbad. It has a room that's more than a mile long with a ceiling two hundred fifty feet above the floor."

Matt blurted out, "That's a commercial cave, lighted and filled with tourists. This is wild. The way caves were meant to be. Let's make the most of it."

Matt turned to Annie. "There's nothing to worry about. I'll be on one side of you. Ginny on the other."

Ginny's cold green eyes blinked lazily. To Annie, she looked like a frog toying with a bug before devouring it.

"Feed the rope slowly through your breaking hand," Matt said to Annie. "And let your sling act as your safety loop. Remember, the front rope is for balance. The back rope controls the rate of descent."

Matt checked Annie's chock and harness. "Stay close to the surface, Annie. You don't have to impress anyone by doing big leaps and bounds. Take your time. Slow and controlled. Twenty yards a minute, max."

To Annie, Matt sounded reassuring and confident, just like her instructor at the spelunkers' club.

Determined to show Ginny they were equals, Annie gritted her teeth and backed toward the edge. She stopped, sucked in her breath, and leaned back against the rope. Letting the rope slide between her hands, she lowered her seat below the level of her feet.

"On the count of three," Matt urged, "push off."

Annie looked down. Dr. Winfield and George were rappelling the steep surface. Following their movements, Annie concentrated. *Push off. Loosen the rope hold. Drop down. Good. Grip the rope tightly and swing into the wall. Push off again.*

To Annie's right, Ginny hung in her sling. "Simple as sitting in a seat," Ginny said. A small smile lifted the corners of her mouth. "On a roller coaster."

"One . . . Two!" Matt shouted.

Annie swallowed over the lump in her throat.

"Three!"

Annie closed her eyes and pushed off. Knees sprung, feet flying, she swung out wildly and whirled in, crashing against the side of the cave. She shook her head back and saw the jagged rim sticking out like the tongue of a prehistoric monster. Trembling, she began her descent into the monster's jaws.

"Relax into your sling," Matt said.

Annie repeated to herself: *Push off, swing out, feed the rope, break, return.* She looked down. Dr. Winfield and George had reached the bottom. They stood nonchalantly between a stalagmite and a column as if they were waiting for a bus. "Come on down!" Their voices reverberated off the walls of the cave.

"You're doing fine," Matt said, timing his descent to Annie's.

Push off, swing out, feed the rope, break, return. Whew! She managed that one without doing damage to herself or the cave.

Push off, swing out, feed the rope, break, return. Two or three more times and, with any luck, she'd reach the bottom.

She couldn't remember being as thankful as she was at that moment when her feet touched the rocky floor. Her legs shook like Gram's strawberry preserves. Perspiration rolled down her back.

"A magnificent cave," Dr. Winfield said. "As dramatic as any I've seen. Just look at these helictites." Annie tried to concentrate as he pointed to the delicate, twisted, hairlike spiral forms that appeared to grow up, down, and sideways. Dr. Winfield rubbed his hands together. "We don't often see this fat, wormlike variety."

George nodded, making notations in his journal. "Annie, I'll want shots of these draperies." He pointed his pen at the curving, translucent speleothem sheets folded over the base of the rim. "They're small, only two to three inches thick, but they'll do."

When the lights had been set up and turned on, Annie couldn't believe her eyes. She had never been below the rim. And she had never seen the cave illuminated except by an ordinary flashlight. With rapid-fire precision, she worked methodically, pivoting from the center of the cave, completing a full circle of photographs at ground level, then going around again at a higher point.

Annie had noticed the excellent physical shape and endurance of the A-Team. On the hike to the cave, Annie observed them with an artist's eye. Dr. Winfield's leg muscles flexed as he sprinted across the bluffs. Ginny's back muscles strained against her shirt as she lifted equipment. George's upper arms tensed, the veins bulging, as he hauled gear. She was even more impressed now as she watched their climbing skills.

Like the advanced students in her spelunkers' club, Dr. Winfield, George, Ginny, and Matt used the two-footed Texas self-belay ascending technique. She watched Matt. He attached both feet to a descender. His left hand held on to a grip that enabled him, by locking and unlocking it, to make his way up the fixed rope. His right hand was hooked to a descender that was affixed to the seat harness. With such a mobile advantage, Matt hung free from the rim. Swinging left and right, crisscrossing the face of the cliff, Matt checked for hidden ledges and hiding places.

Thankfully, Annie stood on solid ground. Several times she noticed Matt and Ginny working side by side. With catlike grace they swung across the walls of the cave. They bypassed jutting rocks and ducked beneath stalactites that hung from the rim. Annie held her breath as Matt and Ginny circumnavigated a wide, jagged edge, then reached out their arms and steadied each other. *Lots of touching going on up there.* Annie winced.

When Ginny and Matt returned to the cave floor, Annie saw Ginny caressing Matt's arm. Jealousy stabbed Annie's heart as Ginny wiped dirt smudges from Matt's face. Annie remembered Tom kidding about all the women who chased Matt around Grayrocks, but he never mentioned their names. To Annie, those were faceless, shadowy personalities, as unreal as paper dolls. But Ginny was real—redheaded, attractive, intelligent, and here—making a play for Matt. And Matt seemed to enjoy her advances.

Annie focused on the changeover of equipment. Having done all they could with the self-belay technique, Matt and the A-Team switched to featherweight, collapsible ladders. They hooked several of the ladders together by their steel cables for extra height and propped them against the rock face. Annie's eyes never left Matt as he began climbing next to Ginny. Annie gasped several times as the ladders shifted and threatened to topple over. Ginny quickly gained the lead, showing off her climbing skills. Her breathy laughter floated down the side of the cave and drove Annie wild. Too nervous and angry to watch, Annie willed herself to take more photographs and immersed herself in her own work.

At noon, Dr. Winfield said, "We've been over the entire area below the rim, and we've struck out. Let's return to the rim and take a quick lunch break. Then we'll look for any secrets hidden up there."

Annie dreaded the ascent. Any ascent, from her experiences with the climbing club, she knew would be more strenuous and difficult than the descent. She hooked herself into her self-belay gear. Trying to keep up with the others and ignoring Ginny's scowls, she inched her way up the rock face toward the rim.

Exhausted, Annie mustered every ounce of her strength and, with help from Matt, struggled over the edge onto the rim. She staggered and collapsed to her knees. Gulping several mouthfuls of air, she gradually felt her breath return to normal. She was surprised that everyone else had similar problems.

"We need some refreshment," Dr. Winfield said.

"We're very near Table Rock," Annie said. "We could have lunch there." She pointed at a formation of rocks, one large, flat rock resting on four smaller ones. They were located halfway around the rim in the deepest recesses of the cave, directly opposite the entrance.

Sitting in a circle around the rock, everyone devoured sandwiches, raisins, and nuts. George wiped his glasses. "Geeze! Look at that," he said. "The designs on the wall change direction immediately above us, dead center over Table Rock."

Dr. Winfield said, "This could be significant. Annie, photograph this area next. We'll prepare the ladders and ropes and pick up our treasure hunt here."

Annie climbed onto Table Rock. When she bent down for an angle shot, she grazed her knee against the rock. Her wound opened up, and blood trickled down her leg.

Annie reached for the first-aid kit, but she lost her balance and knocked it over, spilling the contents. A tube of salve rolled under Table Rock. As she groped under the rock, she felt a cool rush of air.

"Matt, Dr. Winfield, over here! Ginny, George, I've found something. I think it's a tunnel."

Chapter Eleven

"Heave! . . . Ho!" Dr. Winfield groaned.

Everyone pushed. Table Rock shifted, slid back, tilted up, and came to rest on the two rear stones that had supported it. A huge gaping hole materialized below the A-Team.

"Annie's right. It *is* a tunnel." Matt peered into the opening, which was twice the width of his shoulders.

"This could be what we're looking for," Dr. Winfield said. "Matt, the first honor is yours."

Matt lowered himself into the opening. Annie held her breath as he dropped from sight.

"Come on down!" Matt's voice echoed around the cave walls. "It's a small chamber, about ten feet high, twenty feet wide. You won't believe your eyes."

One after the other, Dr. Winfield, Ginny, and George scrambled through the tunnel. Annie was the last to touch down. The sight took her breath away. Beams from their headlights shone on baskets of wampum beads that were stacked everywhere in the musty circular room. Hundreds of baskets. Thousands of beads. White beads, purple beads, dyed beads, beads that the Montauks had slaved to produce for enemy tribes and the white man.

"A wampum supermarket," George marveled.

"Looks like the Montauks played their own game of hide-and-seek," Ginny added.

"And we're *it,*" Matt said. He and Ginny laughed at their little joke.

Jealousy cut through Annie like a knife.

George beamed his light on the ceiling and pushed aside the thick network of cobwebs that clung together like a tapestry.

"Wow!" Annie exclaimed. "It's a painting of Mother Earth, the corn goddess. Exactly like Donald described it to us." Mother Earth, dressed in a turquoise robe, loomed overhead. She held out a cobalt blue basket overflowing with golden corn pollen.

"And there's Father Sky, the corn god," Annie exclaimed as the beam of her light scanned the ceiling. She gasped in amazement at the majestic Father Sky, dressed in a dazzling white and black robe, surrounded by the sun, the moon, and the stars.

"That explains the baskets over there," George said pointing toward the far corner. Corn. An emergency supply in case they had to hide out."

"Photograph everything, Annie," Dr. Winfield

said. "Then we'll move the baskets around and see if there're any surprises underneath."

What a beehive of activity! Kneeling on the floor, Annie began taking pictures. George and Ginny mapped the area. Matt and Dr. Winfield noted the locations. Annie climbed up and down the rungs of her collapsible ladder, snapping rolls and rolls of film. She shot each basket of beads from every possible angle. Then she photographed the finds—arrowheads, tomahawks, bundles of oak sticks, pieces of a fiber blanket.

While the group busied themselves tagging their finds, Annie examined the artwork on the walls. Intrigued by the paintings of birds circling above the wampum, she ran her hands along the wall and followed the path of the winged creatures. She climbed from the rough-slab floor to craggy ledges. She established a foothold and then climbed higher.

"Wait for me, Annie," Matt said. "You know the first rule of caving. Never explore alone."

"Go on after her, Matt," Dr. Winfield said. "The rest of us will stay here and sift through the wampum beads. We'll let you know if we find the dee . . ." The words died out.

"Not so loud," Matt whispered. "Annie might hear. Then we'll have some real hard explaining to do."

The whispered words rattled back and forth, bouncing off the hard surfaces. They stung Annie's ears. Minutes ago, caught up in the excitement of the discoveries, she had felt like a member of the A-Team. Now she felt like an outsider. The more she thought about Dr. Winfield and Matt's secretiveness, the angrier she became. They expected her to show them everything. Yet they were holding back.

Matt hoisted himself onto the ledge and followed the narrow path of chiseled steps that traveled from the wall of the chamber into a tunnel. "Annie, wait up!" His voice boomed into the void where the beam of her light traveled.

Annie decided to play along and see if she could find out their secret. "I think the Montauks chiseled these steps with tools," she said. Her voice remained steady and controlled. She didn't betray her anger, hurt feelings, and twinge of fear.

"It could be an escape route," Matt said. "But the way it twists and turns, I can't figure where it will take us."

"We must be approaching the heart of the cliffs."

"Speaking of hearts, mine's beating very fast," he said. "It must be because I'm close to you."

Annie reached back and squeezed Matt's arm. Maybe he'd admit something if she led him on. *Tell me your secret,* she wanted to say, but she willed herself to silence.

The path veered sharply, and they entered a huge chamber. Beyond the range of their lights, everything was black, the impenetrable black from the void of deepest space. From the echo of their voices, they knew the chamber was large, even larger than Hidden Cave.

"Stay close to the wall," Matt warned. "We could get lost in here."

Hesitantly, following the bird paintings on the wall, they came upon ashes, kindling wood, and the crumbling remains of leather water pouches that lay scattered on the floor.

"This must have been the living quarters for the entire tribe when they hid out," Matt said.

"Darn!" Annie stubbed her toe on a large step and stumbled. "The pathway of stairs continues over here. Let's follow it to the end."

Annie ducked into a narrow tunnel that ascended steeply. Matt followed. In single file, they moved slowly, their arms leading the way as they clung to the slimy, unyielding wall.

"Do you hear that whistling noise?" Matt asked.

"The wind, muffled by something?" Annie surmised. "Or . . ." She laughed. "The ghosts of bootleggers calling to us?"

"Wind," Matt assured her. "It's mixed with the distant sound of water pounding against rock. Ghosts don't whistle, Annie. They moan, like lovesick Romeos, just before capturing their victims." He grabbed her waist and pulled her back into his arms. He kissed the back of her neck and worked his way around to her cheek.

Annie turned around in the cramped space and circled her arms around Matt's neck. She hated to lead him on. It seemed dishonest, but she wanted to know what secret he and Dr. Winfield were keeping from her. "The ghosts of lovesick Juliets have their methods, too." Annie pushed back her hat, tilted her face, and kissed Matt.

As soon as her lips met his, whistling noises, louder than before, reverberated off the walls. Clicks and rattles mingled with the whistles. Long-drawn-out buzzlike screams followed. "We had better get going," she said, pulling away and moving forward.

As they inched along, the tunnel turned sharply back on itself again.

"I think there's light up ahead, but it's faint," Annie said. "The tunnel's steep and narrow. We may have to belay. Take a look."

She ducked down, and Matt peered over her head. "We'll chimney our way up," he said.

"Here goes," Annie said. She placed her feet as high up on the wall as she could and pushed her back firmly against the opposite wall. With one hand on each wall and her toes providing holding power, she squirmed upward. Matt followed, encouraging her with each progression.

"Ugghh!" Annie shouted as she reached a plateau barely half the size of the floor of her tent. "There are bird droppings everywhere."

"Maybe it's bat guano," Matt said. "That can be knee-deep and no fun to slog through. Slippery, smelly . . ."

"Okay, Matt. I get the picture, and it isn't pretty," Annie said.

"Sshhhh," he whispered. "I hear something. Whir-ring noises."

Silence, followed by the drip, drip, of the water from the walls and ceiling.

"Just your imagination," she said, and began to chimney further.

"The tunnel's coming to an end," she said. "There's a ledge just above my shoulders. And there's light, but I can't see where it's coming from." She hoisted herself up and stepped into a small, sloping chamber. Dust particles floated in the pale light.

Suddenly, whirling dark shapes came at Annie from all sides. She closed her eyes and batted her arms over her head. Loud, chattering twitters, magnified by the cave's walls, bombarded her ears. Dropping to her knees, she screamed so loudly that her throat ached.

"It's birds, just common, everyday swifts," Matt said, scrambling to her side. He braced his hands beneath her trembling arms.

The swifts whirled in a huge circle and funneled down toward the cave floor. Annie opened her eyes and saw their short tails and their long, narrow curved wings darting this way and that. They flew toward the ceiling and disappeared. "They nest in the chamber," he said. "We've disturbed their home."

"How did they get in . . . and out?" Annie's voice wavered.

There was enough light now that they turned off their headlights. As their eyes became accustomed to the dimness, they made out the vast interior of the chamber.

"Well, look at that," Matt said. A huge tree, white

as sun-bleached bone, with twigs, stones, and feathers clinging to its mossy, decayed roots, dangled into the cave. It hung there, tipped like a seesaw, about twenty feet above their heads. The limbs were not visible. It was as if they had disappeared into the ceiling of the cave.

Matt aimed his light at the spot where the tree and the cave joined together. "There was a tree like this in the legend Donald told us. Remember? A jealous chief uprooted it, and a sky woman appeared."

He checked out the tree from different angles. "Let's see how stable it is." He slipped a knot into the end of the rope that hung from his waist. "Yippee-yi, kai-yee!" he shouted. The rope spun into the air, then lassoed a protruding rock to the right of the tree.

"You must think you're in the Wild West," Annie teased.

"The West isn't wild anymore, Annie. Caves and racetracks, those are the new frontiers." He tugged the rope, testing the tree. It held.

After several hand-over-hand pulls and a few pushes off the wall to gain momentum, Matt glided through the air. He landed on the tree. "Ride 'em, cowboy, get along l'il doggie," he said, straddling the trunk and whipping his rope free from the rock that had anchored it. "That's the way we used to talk when the tourists came to the dude ranch." He laughed as he tied the rope around the tree. He dropped the end down to Annie.

"You remind me of Donald Eagleton," Annie said,

grabbing the dangling rope. "You make fun of tourists just because they still believe in diehard stereotypes. Are you sure you don't have Indian blood in you?" She grappled with the rope and inched her way toward the top. Matt hoisted her into the air and pulled her up.

"I've got you," Matt said. He reached down, put his arms around Annie's waist, and helped her straddle the tree trunk. They sat facing each other. Hot and tired, they took off their hats and gloves and wiped the perspiration from their faces.

"Annie," Matt blurted out, "I haven't been completely honest with you. There's something I need to tell you."

Let it be that secret, Annie told herself. She wanted to believe Matt Revington.

"My interest in this expedition isn't quite as simple as I made out. What I told you in the beginning is true. I *am* trying to prove myself to my father so that he'll back me as a racer. But there's more . . ."

Annie leaned forward.

"You guessed part of it yourself, Annie. I *am* like Donald Eagleton. I have Indian blood in me."

"I never heard that the Revingtons were part Indian."

"Let me give you the genealogy," Matt said. "In the late seventeen hundreds, my great-grandfather's great-grandfather married a Manhasset named Falling Star. Their son married Eagle Feather, a Shinnecock. History repeated itself, and in 1831 their son married a Shinnecock named Running Deer. That was two years before the Montauks migrated to Wisconsin."

Annie's eyes opened wide. *Running Deer, that's the 'dee' Dr. Winfield and Matt were talking about in the cave.* "Your Indian heritage is one of the best-kept secrets in Grayrocks," Annie said.

"I'm proud of that heritage, Annie. So are my father and uncle. But rich and successful Indians don't fit the Grayrocks's stereotype about Revingtons. So the locals keep pinning other labels on us. Like land-grabbers and bootleggers. It's because I'm Indian that I have a special interest in this expedition. But I can't tell you everything."

"Yes, you can. Tell me right now." The forcefulness of Annie's words surprised her.

"Not yet, Annie. I need a few more days to work out some missing pieces of the puzzle."

"What puzzle?" Annie asked.

"I don't want to alarm you. But if I tell you the rest too soon, your life could be in danger. And so could mine."

"Matt, you're scaring me."

"You're not in any immediate danger," Matt said. "As long as you don't tell the A-Team anything that you don't tell me."

"Are you suggesting that Ginny or George or Dr. Winfield would hurt us?"

"Trust me, Annie. Please trust me for just a few more days. That's the most important thing in the world to me right now."

"I want to trust you, more than anything. But you're asking me to go on blind faith."

"It's too dangerous." Matt took her hands in his. "But I'll tell you this much. I need to find the treasure that's hidden in these caves before anyone else does."

"It could be anywhere," Annie said.

"No. The people who hid it wanted it found. By the right person."

His voice was so sincere, his eyes so pleading. Those eyes—those eyes couldn't lie to her.

Matt held Annie's face in his hands. He kissed her mouth, lingering with a meaning beyond mere words. His warm lips caressed her cheeks, her eyes, her hair. He whispered in her ear, "Please, Annie, be on my side. Help me."

"I . . . I need to think."

He kissed her again and again.

She felt herself melting in his arms. She pushed away. "I'm confused, Matt. Let me sort things out."

"Promise?" he asked, and kissed her again.

"I won't have any private talks with the A-Team. Not today. I'll give you today."

"Thanks, Annie. One day at a time. That's all I can ask for." He turned abruptly. "Did you hear something?" he asked. "Maybe I'm spooked, but I could swear I heard Ginny's voice."

"That's not Ginny. It's cackling birds." Annie laughed. "Look behind you. You'll see how they get in and out of here."

Matt and Annie crawled up the trunk toward a small patch of blue sky. Leaning away from the trunk, they pulled away the loose soil on either side of the tree. Carefully, they tugged at the earth. The tree, wedged into the opening, began to teeter. Warm air blew on their cheeks. Suddenly, a large chunk of earth came away in Matt's hands and fell to the floor of the cave. He poked his head and shoulders through the opening.

"Hey, we're on the cliffs overlooking the water," he said. His voice was filled with excitement. "This must have been the Montauks' lookout. From here they could spot anyone coming for miles away."

Annie looked through the opening, her face brushing Matt's. She saw that the overcast morning had vanished into the dappled afternoon sunshine. Waves crashed against the base of the cliffs. From their high perch, boulders on the beach looked like fist-sized stones. The view was dizzying.

Annie said, "All the times I've looked at these cliffs from the sea, I never realized a network of caves lay hidden within." She looked up. "We're near the top of the cliffs. There's patches of soil and trees up here. Do you suppose this tree blew down during a hurricane and lodged in here?"

"Could be," Matt said. "Or maybe a sky woman brought it here. We'll never know."

They ducked their heads back into the cave. Matt kissed Annie again, more passionately than before. Her defenses were dropping away. "Did you feel the earth move?" he asked.

"Maybe the tree shifted." She laughed.

Swifts flew near the opening, then dropped from

view, only to reappear moments later on air currents. They beat the air with rapid wing beats and chattered loudly at Annie and Matt, who were blocking the entrance to their nests.

My dream, she thought, *the birds. Could there be some connection between the birds and the treasure? There must be.* She felt it so strongly.

"Those swifts seem to have upset you," Matt said.

"Remember? I told you those birds were in my dream."

"Tell me again," he said.

"The birds flew into something round like this hole." Annie stopped short. Why hadn't she thought of it sooner? As clearly as she saw waves pummel the shore, she knew, for certain, where the treasure was hidden. She had an overwhelming urge to return to Grayrocks and check out her parents' photos of Hidden Cave. "We had better get back to the others," she said. "We can talk about it later."

"The others have come to you," came a voice from below. Matt and Annie jumped. George's head and shoulders emerged from the tunnel.

"Well, well, well," Ginny said, following on George's heels, "if it isn't the lovebirds, perched in a tree. There's work to be done in case you forgot."

Chapter Twelve

Dr. Winfield twirled a birch switch over the campfire, savoring the aroma of toasting marshmallow. "I'm proud of the progress we made in Hidden Cave today, but we need to work faster. Here's my plan for tomorrow. Come dawn, Ginny, George, Matt, and I will haul the beads and other finds back to camp. Annie will return to Grayrocks, pick up supplies, and run errands. Then she'll come back here as quickly as possible to process the finds. And remember, Annie"—Dr. Winfield stopped to inspect the charred blob—"I want your parents' cave photos." His words sounded like a threat. Return with the photos or else.

"Annie, how about a swim before dark?" Matt suggested when they were alone.

"Sure." She was glad to get away from the A-Team for a while.

"Meet me at the dock."

Annie dropped her towel, and Matt saw her poised in her tomato-red bathing suit. Annie couldn't help but notice his admiration. She was thrilled by his lean, muscular body, his firm stomach, the way his navy trunks rode low over his slim hips.

Annie felt warm and tingly running beside Matt along the beach toward the cliffs. The sun slid below the horizon. A cool breeze blew on their faces and whipped the choppy water. They dived into the water and swam toward the boulders a half mile offshore. Cold, exhilarating, the water sprayed over them as they swam, sending up bubbles, like clusters of diamonds that soared toward the sky. Annie and Matt clung to the boulders and to each other as the bubbling spray washed away their fatigue and aching muscles. Like playful kids, they slipped beneath the water, grabbed each other by the hands, and shot up into the foaming waves.

They swam back to shore, dragged along by currents toward the dark, imposing cliffs. Matt pulled Annie past the breaking waves. Hand in hand, they struggled through the churning surf onto the sand. They slid into each other's arms as they collapsed, and the tide ebbed and flowed around them. They kissed. Annie felt the world around her disappear as he caressed her shoulders, back, and waist. Touching him sent chills through her. *So this was what love*

*felt like. This was what books and movies and her
friends had been telling her about.* She closed her
eyes.

More than anything Annie wanted Matt Revington
to care for her. But confusion overwhelmed her. She
pulled back, pushed him away. "No. It's too fast,"
she said. "Please try to understand. I want to trust
you, but this secrecy . . . I can't. I just can't."

"I'm sorry, Annie. I got caught up in the moment.
It was a mistake. We need to finish the project. That
has to be our priority."

Matt turned onto his back, and for a long time they
lay in the sand, the outgoing tide lapping at their feet.
Side by side, they held hands and watched the moon
rise over the cliffs and cast purple shadows on the
sand. Darkness enveloped them. Black feathery
clouds swirled across the moon. The foghorns of two
distant ships moaned their lonesome warnings, then
passed on the dark sea. The foghorns sounded once
more, then faded away.

Annie remembered a thick blanket of fog and pelting rain. A slippery incline. Headlights on the glistening black road. There was a car at the bottom of
a gully, then total blackness and a cold numbness.
She recalled the sudden silence, the blood flowing
from her forehead, arms, and legs.

Matt touched her arm.

"I remember something horrible about Mom and
Dad's accident." Annie sat up, and the new, disturb-
ing memory of the accident retreated. "I need to talk
to Gram."

"There's someone else you should talk to. When you get to Grayrocks, call my aunt Arabelle. She'll be expecting your call. She'll tell you something you need to know about your parents."

"What about them?" Annie grew uneasy.

"About the accident."

Panic raced through Annie. "Matt, please tell me."

He kissed her tenderly on the eyes. "This isn't the time or place." He brushed away her tears and held her close.

When they stood, Annie felt as if the world were spinning out of control, that she was swirling down, into a dark abyss, that her heart might break into a thousand pieces. Slowly, they walked back to camp. George was waiting for them by the campfire.

"Matt, how about some poker? Just you and me and Dr. Winfield."

"Sure," Matt said.

As Annie tried to fall asleep, she heard cards being shuffled, bits and pieces of the men's conversations, and coins clinking. When the game finally broke up, she peered past the flap of her tent. Were her eyes playing tricks? George's hand darted across the blanket and stole a stack of coins from Matt. Before she could blink, George grabbed a handful of coins from Dr. Winfield too. *Why, that little thief,* Annie thought as she rolled over and closed her eyes.

Unable to sleep, Annie peered out again. In the waning firelight of the chilly night, Matt sat cross-legged on a blanket, dressed in jeans and a flannel shirt, his dark hair falling forward on his face. He riffled through the Polaroid pictures of the cave, pulled out several for a closer look, then put them away. He took a harmonica from his pocket. He stretched out his long legs and, resting on one elbow, played the saddest tunes Annie had ever heard. The sadness felt so real, she wanted to reach out and hold it in her hands in its pure essence before it mingled with the smoke from the campfire, spiraled into the air, floated across the moon, then moved on, free to choose its own path before being swallowed by the night.

She closed her eyes. A distant ship's foghorn moaned again. A sick feeling rose in her stomach. Visions of the car crash broke through her thoughts. She remembered struggling out of the car and crawling up a cliff toward the road. A loud noise. An explosion. She looked back. More explosions. Flames consumed her parents' car, and metal scraps flew skyward. Even now, after all this time, her eyes smarted at the memory, and her throat tightened over a strangled sob. In the depths of despair, Annie surrendered to her grief. They'd still be alive today if only . . . She clenched her hands into fists and sobbed into her pillow.

Suddenly, Matt knelt beside her in the tent. He cradled her in his arms. "What's this crying all about?" he asked.

"Matt," she began, but could only sob.

"There's no reason for either of us to be lonely or alone," he murmured as he nestled beside her. In the pitch-blackness, she listened to his steady breathing. She felt safe. Before drifting into a deep sleep, she saw his hands intertwined with hers beneath the moonlight. A sweet tenderness engulfed her, warming her entire being. She longed to trust Matt completely, to believe that they might have a future together.

Several times Annie stirred. She thought she heard the muffled sounds of an engine farther down the beach, near the cliffs. *It's only a dream,* she told herself. *No one would be arriving or leaving Big Shell Island in the middle of the night.*

After docking *Island Hoppers* at the marina, Annie tried to complete her errands as quickly as possible, but the Grayrocks business district was swarming. Tourists darted everywhere, on foot, in cars, on rollerblades, on bikes. The hullabaloo of high season was going full blast.

Raucous locals, eager to feed the Grayrocks grapevine, greeted Annie. "How you been?" . . . "Where you been?" . . . "Who the heck you been there with?" They punctuated the air with growls and scampered around Annie on all fours. This was their insiders' joke, their response to tourists who claimed that the people of Grayrocks hibernated like bears during the winter and came out to play in the summer. Going along with the joke, Annie pawed at Nell, Ed, Jake, and several other shop owners. She joined in the fun of telling tall tales, the kind that brought the tourists and their money back year after year.

With effort, Annie bought the watertight packing crates Dr. Winfield wanted. She mailed the film to Andrews University to be developed, "away from the prying eyes of Grayrocks," as Dr. Winfield insisted. And she called Gram, who promised to prepare food immediately and ask questions later. Finally, Annie ended up in a phone booth at the Corner Cafe. She held a cup of Sally's steaming coffee in one hand and, in the other, a piece of paper on which Matt had written Arabelle Revington's unlisted phone number.

"Hello. My name is Annie Devane. May I please speak to Matthew Revington's aunt, Arabelle Revington?" *No, too formal.* "Hi. Mrs. Revington? I'm Annie Devane, a friend of Matt's." Annie practiced the words she would say to the reclusive Arabelle Revington, the mystery woman she'd never seen, the woman who owned one of her paintings.

Annie checked her watch. It was nine forty-five. Sally and the other waitresses were laughing and clawing the air with their long red nails. They scooped honey into pots to serve to tourists along with their muffins and toast.

Sam Tibbs, one of the regulars, tapped on the glass panel of the phone booth. "Annie, if you're meditating, you should be staring at your navel. If you're going to make a call, you need to pick up the receiver."

Annie waved Sam away and put a quarter in the slot. She dialed the number.

"Annie?" a soft, sultry voice asked.

"Yes," Annie replied, startled.

"I've been expecting your call. My husband, David, let me know you had arrived. He saw you dock at the marina. Please come for brunch. Have your grandmother drive you here. I'd like her to hear what I have to say too. And I'd like to keep our meeting confidential."

"Annie"—Sally motioned her toward the counter with a dishtowel—"Tom just called from the marina. He says two men are nosing around, asking lots of questions about Big Shell Island. They want to charter a boat and go there tomorrow. Tom spoke without thinking, told them you were taking *Island Hoppers* there this afternoon. The more Tom talked to the guys, the less he liked them. He covered, made an excuse that *Island Hoppers* will be too full of supplies for passengers. He reserved a boat for them tomorrow afternoon and a room at Gram's for tonight."

Annie shook her head. "I don't like Tom's putting Gram in danger."

"It's okay," Sally said. "Tom will stay at the inn with Gram and see what he can find out. And Annie, one more thing. Tom said Matt had warned him earlier that some people, land developers or something, might want to sabotage his expedition. Tom wants you to get word to Matt as soon as possible. He owes Matt that. And more."

The cold, clammy hand of fear raced up and down Annie's spine. "Did Tom say what the guys looked like?"

"Yeah. City types. Says they're dressed in touristy clothes that their maids must have ironed. Annie, what's happening on Big Shell Island? What are you and Matt up to?"

Gram nudged the refrigerator door shut with her hip and tossed another handful of chopped carrots into a tub of coleslaw. "Two well-dressed bad guys staying here for the night? Won't be the first time. I can handle them." Gram winked. "Brunch with Arabelle Revington? That's special. I wouldn't miss it for the world. Except for a few workmen, none of us locals have ever been inside her home." She slid the tub of coleslaw across the counter. "Come on. Your Shell Island catering service is officially on break."

Annie snapped shut the album that contained her parents' photos of Hidden Cave. She'd seen enough. The treasure had been right under their noses all along. She tucked the album in the kitchen cabinet behind the sacks of flour. "Let's go!" she said.

Gram backed Baywatch Inn's pickup truck out of the driveway. "We're on the road again," she sang off-key. Annie tried hard to match Gram's cheerfulness, but before the truck came to the first intersection, she broke into tears.

"What's the matter, Annie?" Gram handed her some tissues. "Oh, I know what's wrong. You're torn every which way about Matt Revington."

Annie sniffled and blew her nose. "It's more than that, Gram. I've had some bad dreams, memories actually, about the accident."

The creases between Gram's eyes deepened. "I've been expecting this for a long time. The doctors warned me that repressed memories can be traumatic when they're eventually recalled. You've kept your feelings bottled up ever since that horrible night. Let them out. Tell me about the memories."

"The first part I already knew, that Mom and Dad were on their way home from an S.O.S. meeting. They picked me up at Sally and Tom's, where I had been baby-sitting their Bobby. I fell asleep in the backseat. Noises, I remember so many noises. Squealing brakes. Screeching tires and metal grinding. We careened through the guardrail. I was slammed against the roof. We landed in a grove of trees. My head was filled with buzzing. Mom and Dad . . ." She sobbed.

"Go on, Annie, tell me the new memories. You'll feel better."

Annie swallowed hard. "I remember shaking Mom and Dad. I couldn't get them to wake up. I went for help, but I shouldn't have. If only I had dragged them from the car first, they'd still be alive today. It's all my fault."

"Stop right there, Annie. You did everything possible. You were in shock. You were weak and losing blood. You couldn't have pulled them from the car. You're lucky the explosion didn't kill you too."

Gram pulled the truck to the side of the road and turned off the engine. Annie collapsed into her arms, sobbing. "Your mom and dad are smiling down from heaven right now," Gram said. "They're happy that you're alive. They're proud of everything you've done with your life."

"Do you really think so?" Annie blubbered into Gram's neck.

"Absolutely."

"But Gram, I miss them so much. I can't stop thinking about the special times we shared. Our picnics, Dad's funny magic tricks, the way Mom brushed my hair." She sobbed bitterly. "Their lives were cut short. And I'll always feel responsible."

"Listen to me. It will take time, but you need to realize that it's not your fault. You didn't cause the accident." Gram hugged Annie and kissed her on the cheek. "No one, not you or anyone else, is responsible. It was an accident. Your mom and dad wouldn't want you to feel bad, would they?"

"No." Annie sniffled.

"As for these memories, I don't have the right medical jargon. But I think your mind and your heart got tired of fighting each other and called a truce." Gram patted Annie on the knee. She turned the key in the ignition and steered the truck onto the road.

Chapter Thirteen

As Annie looked through the open window of the truck, the black, silent, slow-motion world of despair released its grip. The colors and sounds of summer were everywhere. Hollyhocks and hydrangeas peeked through white fences along Portside Road. Forsythia bushes captured the buttery yellow of the sun. Hummingbirds whirred their wings near the honeysuckle vines clinging to porch rails.

Annie envied the barefoot boys in bathing suits who rolled their inner tubes along the sidewalk. She delighted at the sight of two little girls dressed up in their mommies' frills, high heels, and straw hats, giggling on their front-porch swing. Mrs. Abbot and the bridge ladies, cards held to their bosoms, set down their iced-tea glasses to wave to Gram from their wicker and chintz perches.

133

"Mom and Dad loved summer days like this," Annie said. A bittersweet nostalgia overwhelmed her. She couldn't begin to label the emotions sweeping over her. "Everything special happens in summer, they used to say." She wanted to act on impulse and live for the moment. But since the accident, something had always pulled her back and held her in its clutches. Until today, she hadn't been able to define that something any more than she could tear herself from its grip. Now stirrings deep within her made her realize that guilt, transformed into an impenetrable numbness, had kept her heart and feelings locked in ice. Burdened by her guilt, she had found one excuse after another not to love Matt Revington. She would begin by trusting him.

Gram continued driving and listened while Annie described her experiences on Big Shell Island and her feelings about Matt. Gram grew silent for a long while, then mused aloud: "Annie, I don't believe Matt has a dishonest bone in his body. He wouldn't hurt you or anyone else. If he's keeping secrets from you, he has a good reason. Look at it from his point of view. You say he suspects there's a possible troublemaker in your group, that some land-grabbers from New York City want to sabotage the expedition. He probably doesn't want to involve you until he's sure what's going on and you'll be safe."

"You make it sound so simple and logical, Gram. I want so much to trust him."

"You're all I have in this world, and your safety concerns me. I'm worried about these two snoopy guys who're trying to get to Big Shell Island. I'll put in a word with my good friend Hank. We go way back, further than either of us likes to admit, even before he was the chief of police. He'll manage to detain these guys." She laughed. "He'll drag them into the station and let the boys in blue have some fun questioning them about breaking the Grayrocks dress code. Why, I'll bet those city slickers have creases in their pants and wear matching socks." They both laughed.

Gram stopped at the last traffic light in Grayrocks and entered East Bay, an area of prestigious homes on Long Island Sound. "Annie, go back to Matt and help him find the buried treasure. But play it safe. Don't let the A-Team suspect you're in cahoots with Matt. Show them your cool ice-princess attitude, the one you practiced on all the young Romeos in Grayrocks. Then get the blazes away from Big Shell Island."

Gram braked and turned into Land's End Lane, known as Revington Road by most people in Grayrocks. She followed the narrow road for five miles, passing several secluded mansions.

"What do you think she'll be like?" Annie asked. "A bad-tempered matron who slurs her words and staggers around with a drink in her hand? A sedated zombie? Those are the rumors spread along the Grayrocks grapevine."

"Maybe she'll surprise us. She could turn out to be a very kind woman. I hear she was treated in a clinic abroad and is still recovering from her last nervous breakdown."

The road ended in a cul-de-sac. Gram slowed down. As if by magic, wrought-iron gates parted. Gram drove through. Annie marveled at the grounds that spread out majestically beyond the high hedge and iron fence. Sculptured flower beds, flanked by rhododendron and protected by towering maples that arched over the lush carpet of lawn, bordered the road. Traveling around the bend, they approached a pale yellow Victorian home, trimmed in white, sprawling in all directions beneath sloping roofs. Across the front, wraparound porches sheltered white wicker chairs and tables evenly spaced beneath hanging pots of ferns. The front door displayed a magnificent frosted window on which was etched a pair of seagulls in flight.

Although Annie knew that Arablele and David Revington had no heirs, she somehow expected to see rosy-cheeked children, dressed in white, playing croquet or flying colorful kites with the tails streaming across the sky. Instead, a stillness hung in the air, expectant, as if waiting for someone to break through the invisible aura that imprisoned the estate and its owners.

Gram drove along the circular brick drive and parked the car near the house. As Annie absorbed all the colors around her, she couldn't help but think that Arabelle had a deep, dark secret to reveal. Both Matt and Arabelle had been guarded about the nature of this visit.

Before Annie had time to ring the bell, a butler opened the door. Arabelle Revington descended the winding staircase and greeted them. Dressed in white silk slacks and blouse, Arabelle was striking. She was younger than Annie expected. She had a small, delicate face with prominent cheekbones, penetrating eyes, perfect even teeth, and a cap of curly hair that framed her face.

"Mrs. Revington," Annie and Gram began, both speaking at the same time.

"Please, call me Arabelle and come this way."

Arabelle led them through the living room. "Lovely," she said, nodding toward *Sea Treasures,* Annie's painting, as she passed through French doors to the porch. The spectacular view of Midnight Point served as a backdrop to the table draped in white linen and set with glistening china and silver.

"We'll have brunch here," Arabelle said when the maid had finished pouring tea. Small talk about the weather led to a history of the house, a discussion about the tourist season at Baywatch Inn, and a description of Annie's fall-semester courses.

Seconds after Arabelle rang a small silver bell, the maid returned. She snapped open a starched napkin and placed it on Arabelle's lap, then repeated the maneuver for Gram and Annie. With an elegant spoon in each hand, she deftly served crab-mushroom omelets, spinach salad, and poppy-seed muffins.

Annie gasped. "I can't believe it. This was my mother's favorite meal. She'd order it in restaurants on her birthday." Annie pressed her fingertips to her temples and frowned. "This can't be a coincidence."

Arabelle put her hand on Annie's arm. "This may surprise you, but your mother sat on that very chair where you're sitting."

Annie's jaw dropped. "You knew my mother?"

"Yes. David always had his photos developed at your parents' shop. Once, when David didn't have time to pick up some important photos, important because they showed him winning a golf tournament at the club, your mother offered to drop them off. She stayed for a cup of tea. She talked about you quite a bit . . . almost as much as Matt does."

Annie shifted in the chair. She felt her cheeks flush.

Arabelle continued. "While you're eating, you might enjoy hearing about another time I spent with your mother. My chauffeur, Stanley, took me for a drive one June day. We passed a car on the side of the road, disabled with a flat tire, and there was your mother." She nodded toward Gram. "Your daughter." She wiped imaginary crumbs from her lap. "Caitlin had a very determined look on her face as she attempted to free a tire iron from the trunk of the car. Stanley rolled up his shirtsleeves and attended to the problem. We sat in the car, discussing everything under the sun. A camaraderie blossomed. I felt it. So did she."

The thought that Arabelle Revington and her mother were friends brought a startled look and then a smile to Annie's face. No two women in the world could be more different than Arabelle Revington and Caitlin Devane.

When Annie and Gram had finished eating, Arabelle shook the bell again. The tinkling sound brought the maid, who cleared the dishes, then left silently, closing the doors behind her.

"Caitlin and I managed to get together as often as possible after that," Arabelle continued. "We enjoyed each other's company. So, when I expressed an interest, she offered to give me photography lessons."

The maid returned with a tray of espresso and strawberry shortcake piled high with whipped cream.

"Caitlin's favorite dessert," Gram remarked as the maid departed.

Arabelle savored a forkful of strawberry shortcake. "We photographed the water, the house, the birds, everything here at Land's End, and we talked. Caitlin's optimistic outlook on life helped me enormously. We shared confidences. My frail nerves are no secret. Caitlin listened to me and offered many practical solutions. She encouraged long walks and meditation." She paused and sipped her espresso. "Friendships are not one-sided. Caitlin confided in me. She felt she was in danger."

Annie and Gram leaned forward in their chairs.

"Danger?" Gram asked, the color draining from her face. "Caitlin was my daughter. If she had been in danger, she would have told me."

"Or me," Annie said.

"She didn't want to alarm either of you," Arabelle said. "Your father, of course, knew."

"Then Andy would have told me," Gram said. "He was my son-in-law, but we were as close as a son and mother. Anyone could tell you—"

"What danger?" Annie interrupted.

"A man, someone they didn't know, came into their camera shop and threatened to hurt them. There were phone calls too. The man wanted your parents to give up their work as publicity chairmen for the Save Our Shells committee. He told them to resign if either were elected president . . . or else."

"What could be so important that they would be threatened? Why, it's outrageous," Annie said.

Gram's hands trembled as she set down her espresso. "Why didn't Caitlin and Andy go to the police? They knew Hank, the chief of police. He would have helped them."

"They planned to as soon as they completed a last batch of photos and fliers, but the accident . . . Well, they never had the chance."

Gram gripped Arabelle's arm. "Do you think that man had anything to do with the accident?"

"It's possible," Arabelle replied. "Caitlin was quite upset the last time I saw her. That's why I'm telling you this."

Annie seethed with anger. "Why didn't you come forward and tell the police what you're telling us? It's been five years."

"David didn't want me to. He said the pressure of a police inquest would be too much for my nerves. He was concerned."

"Concerned?" Gram swallowed hard. "My daughter's dead and all you can think about is that David was concerned?"

"Please." Arabelle cried quietly. "David was right. My nerves can't take this." She took several pills from a silver case and swallowed them.

Annie gripped the edge of the table. "When did Matt find out about this?"

"Not until the night before the expedition. He made me promise that at the first opportunity I would tell you everything in the presence of your grandmother. He didn't want you to be alone when you heard it."

Annie stood. "I must return to Big Shell Island."

Arabelle said, "I'll call David and let him know you're on the way."

Gram said, "Let's keep him out of this. After what I've heard today, I don't trust his judgment. Besides, with his investments in Grayrocks real estate, he has more than a passing interest in the development of the Shell Islands."

Arabelle said, "Surely you don't think David has anything to do with those land thieves who want to put up high-rises on the Shells. He would never—"

"How can you be so sure?" Gram interrupted. "Please don't say anything to him. Please. If your friendship with Caitlin meant anything, you'll help us by keeping quiet."

"Yes," Arabelle said. Her voice trembled. "And now, if you'll excuse me, I must lie down."

* * *

"We'll call Tom," Gram said on the way to Bay-watch Inn. "We'll ask him to keep those two guys snooping around the marina busy while you and *Island Hoppers* take off for Big Shell. And we'll tell Tom to keep David in the dark. We don't know if he can be trusted."

Annie said, "Don't tell Tom or Sally any more than necessary."

"Why?" A startled expression crossed Gram's face.

"Because, better than anyone else, Tom and Sally knew Mom and Dad's schedule that night."

"Tom's done a few underhanded things to get money," Gram said. "He's pocketed Sally's house money and played around with the checkbook, but he's not capable of this. And Sally loved your parents. She couldn't be involved."

"But Gram, you know how Sally defends Tom and makes excuses for him. Let's play it safe for now."

"I'm going to the police," Gram said. "I think someone tampered with the car. That was no accident!"

Annie gasped. "My God!" The color drained from her face. She fought back tears. "Please wait one more day before going to the police. Give me time to talk to Matt and dig up the buried treasure. Let me find out if there's a connection between the treasure and Mom and Dad's deaths and their work with S.O.S."

Annie turned to Gram with troubled eyes. "What could the treasure be?"

"I hope it's a chest filled with cheap junk," Gram replied. She embraced Annie. "The more valuable the treasure and the more desperate someone is to have it, the more your life is in danger."

Chapter Fourteen

Annie's mind churned with questions and theories as she steered *Island Hoppers* toward Big Shell Island. She tried to imagine a man hired by All-Atlantic Associates hiding in Mom and Dad's garage, lifting the hood of the car, tinkering with the engine or messing with the fuel line. Impossible! Not in Grayrocks. Those two men snooping around the marina—were they hired by All-Atlantic Associates? They were headed this way, so they were somehow involved with the treasure. It was all connected. How did Matt fit into any of this?

Tom and Sally couldn't have been desperate enough to get involved with All-Atlantic Associates. Mom and Dad practically raised Sally. Tom was rough, but he had never been in trouble with the law.

Who was the man who came into Mom and Dad's

shop and threatened to hurt them? Mom couldn't have known him or she would have told Arabelle his name along with the other details of the story. Or was Arabelle holding back because the man was involved with David's real-estate ventures?

The A-Team could be mixed up in this. Dr. Winfield was secretive. Ginny was capable of anything. George was under Dr. Winfield's thumb and Ginny's too. The three could be in this together. Safety in numbers. Conspiracy of thieves.

With renewed determination, Annie vowed to uncover the circumstances of her parents' deaths regardless of who was involved. As she approached the dock, one thing remained certain, and it scared her. Once she and Matt had the treasure in their possession, their lives would be in jeopardy.

Annie's afternoon on Big Shell Island was so hectic that she had little time to mull over her nagging thoughts. She photographed, labeled, and recorded the bags of wampum beads and other finds that Matt and the A-Team had hauled from the caves. Then, while Dr. Winfield outlined plans—return to Grayrocks in the morning, transport the finds to Andrews University in the afternoon, return to Big Shell Island the following day to continue their research—she helped pack everything in containers and load them onto *Island Hoppers.*

For the few brief minutes she'd managed to be alone with Matt, she quickly recounted Arabelle's conversation. She was filling him in on Gram's suspicions and Tom's warning when she saw Ginny heading their way.

"Meet me outside Hidden Cave at eight o'clock," Annie whispered to Matt. "Bring a shovel and flashlight. And don't let anyone see you."

"What about rappelling gear?"

"Not necessary."

"Tell me where the treasure's buried," he said.

"You tell me *what* it is, I'll tell you *where* it is."

"Deal. But not now. Later, at the cave."

At seven o'clock, Annie hurried toward Hidden Cave.

"Slowpoke," Matt whispered in the darkness.

"Tell me what's buried here," Annie said, collapsing next to him at the cave's entrance.

"A piece of paper and a belt."

"That's what's putting our lives in danger?"

"Actually, a *land deed* verified with a *wampum* belt," he said. "Research for my master's degree took me to Madison University in Wisconsin to check out some recovered diaries written by a frontiersman named Luke Woodstone. He described the migration of the Montauks to Wisconsin in 1833. His detailed information hadn't been noted in any other correspondence, diaries, or manuscripts or in reports by Indian superintendents."

"Go on. I'm listening," Annie said.

"The Montauks had already decided to move to the reservation in Wisconsin to be close to people who shared their beliefs. The day before the migration, the Montauks met with local officials here on Big Shell. The officials, acting on behalf of the governor, deeded the shells to the Montauks. The Montauks accepted. But since they didn't believe in the concept of ownership, they recommended that the islands be turned into a park for future generations. To augment the white man's scribblings about the transaction, the Montauks made a wampum belt. Actually duplicate sets of the deeds and wampum belts were made. One set for the white men and one for the Montauks."

"And which do you think are buried here?"

"According to the Woodstone diaries," Matt said, "the white men drowned as they returned home from the meeting. Their deed and wampum belt found a watery grave. The Woodstone diaries went on to say that the Montauks placed their deed and belt inside Mother Earth, to be nourished until needed."

"Are you sure it was *this* island?"

"The Woodstone diaries stated clearly that the island had a wall of cliffs. That narrows it to Big Shell."

"Why all the secrecy?" Annie asked.

"We knew that if word leaked out, we'd be swamped with historians and anthropologists, and possibly land-grabbing developers eager to discredit the deed to assure the construction of condos. For Dr. Winfield, it's a matter of professional and local pride. He wants Long Island's Andrews University to beat out Wisconsin's Madison University in publishing the findings. So far, no one from Wisconsin has come here. They didn't get grant money . . . yet."

Matt took Annie's hands in his. "Do you see what's at stake, Annie? We can keep the Shell Islands part of the park system. The wampum belt alone, if the designs back up the sequence of events, might convince a court. There's precedent. If the deed survived, then, of course, we'd have a solid case."

"How come you've taken such an interest in this?" Annie asked. "You're going to be a racer, not an anthropologist."

"A fair question, Annie. Do you remember my telling you about Samuel Revington?"

"The one who married a Manhasset?"

Matt nodded. "I'm convinced Samuel Revington was the local official who signed the deed. He was born in 1780. He was involved in local politics, and he would have been fifty-three in 1833, when the deed was signed. He fits the Woodstone diaries' description of a tall man with sharp features, a jagged scar on the back of his hand, thick black hair flecked with gray, and married to an Indian woman."

Annie shivered in the cold night air. "Does any of your family know about this?"

"My father and uncle. They're behind this project one hundred percent." Matt leaned closer to Annie. "I want to prove that the Revingtons never have been land-grabbers. They were decent people who respected the rights of others. I want to clear the Revington name once and for all. Wouldn't you do the same for your family?"

"Yes," Annie said emphatically. "And I want to find the deed and belt as much as you do. But we need help from the police, and soon. When word spreads that we have the deed and belt, I'm afraid that the people who threatened my parents, maybe even murdered them, are involved in this and will make their move. They're likely to come after us. The police should be brought in."

Matt stood and pulled Annie to her feet. "We'll work this out together."

A light drizzle began.

"I'm sorry I ever doubted you," she said.

"It's all forgotten," he said. "Now tell me, where are the belt and deed buried?"

"If I'm right, and I'm sure I am, you're standing on them."

"You're kidding!" He kicked the sand with his hiking boot. "How'd you figure it out?"

"Donald's words and my dream about circles and birds. The clincher was my parents' photos. They confirmed that this entrance used to be circular and very large."

Matt placed the heel of his boot hard on his shovel and pressed it into the sandy soil. "Let's see if your theory pans out," he said, turning the first shovelful of earth.

Annie dug too, pitching shovelfuls over her shoulder.

The drizzle turned to a light rain.

A half hour later, Matt rested on his shovel and wiped his brow on his shirtsleeve. "Are you still so sure?" he asked.

"Keep digging," she said.

"Slave driver." He resumed shoveling.

"Annie, I've hit something!" He tossed his shovel aside, dropped to his knees, and scooped the sand aside.

"What is it?" Annie leaned into the hole, focusing the flashlight.

"A small wooden chest." His excited voice stirred Annie's blood.

Side by side, they hurriedly removed the remaining sand, freeing the chest. They lifted the chest from the hole and set it down between them. Matt tugged at the lid. It was locked.

"I hate to break the lock," Matt said.

"Give me a shot at it," Annie said. She removed a clip from her hair and jiggled it in the lock. "A trick I learned from my father. He did magic tricks," she added.

Matt tugged at the lid again. The rusty hinges squeaked in protest but finally gave way. Matt and Annie hunched over the chest. Their anticipation reached fever pitch.

A twig snapped behind them. Their flashlights spun a wide beam around them. The frightened eyes of a deer stared back at them.

Matt and Annie blew out their breath and rolled their shoulders.

"Let's hurry," Annie said. "It's spooky here at night."

They shined their flashlights into the chest. A sheepskin pouch and a folded blue blanket lay next to each other. Reverently, Matt lifted the blanket, set it on the ground, and unfolded it.

Annie and Matt gasped. Moonlight glinted off the rainbow-colored beads.

Matt whistled low and long as he unrolled the belt. "It must be six feet."

"Wow!" Annie cried. "It's Mother Earth and Father Sky. Beneath them, their people are holding hands, circling their wigwams and campfires. Why, it's the—"

"Circle of Unity and Friendship."

"Look!" Annie touched the left end of the belt. "The Montauks are pulling the white men's boats ashore."

Matt raced the beam of his flashlight along the design. "The Montauk chief and the white leader are shaking hands."

"And smoking the peace pipe."

"And feasting."

"Over here people are dancing up the corn."

"And playing drums."

"Shaking rattles."

Matt's mouth flew open. "Incredible!" He pointed at the black beads.

"Birds," Annie marveled.

"Messenger birds from the spirit world." Matt's voice trembled with awe.

"They're flying around the sun."

"A sign that the Montauk ancestors approved of the meeting."

Annie peered into the sheepskin pouch. "Two scrolls tied with wampum strings." She kept one and handed the other to Matt.

Matt opened his scroll. Astounded, he sat back on his heels. "Mine's a map of Grayrocks Bay. Latitude, longitude, Big Shell and Little Shell—marked with an X and a Y—Plum Island, Gardiner's Island, Montauk Point, Orient Point." His words tumbled out.

Annie leaned toward Matt and shined her flashlight on the map. "Look at the handwriting at the bottom. Can you believe those fancy flourishes and old-fashioned spelling?"

Matt spread the scroll across his knees and began to read.

"This land deed is presented in good faith to chief sachem, King Pharaoh, on this eighteenth day of this seventh month in the year of our Lord, 1833. It testifies before God and man that the rightful ownership of the two islands designated on the map as X and Y are hereby and forevermore assigned to the Confederated Tribes of the Montauk Indians. Signed by Samuel Revington and Caleb Blackstone, appointed by governor William M. Marcy, the governor of New York, as his representatives in Indian matters. Witnessed by Josiah Rawlings and Andrew

Ferguson, Daniel Crow, and John Running Brook."

Matt's eyes glistened as he traced the signature of Samuel Revington with his index finger.

"Wait till you hear this," Annie said, her eyes wide with awe. "My document's written by King Pharaoh, the grand sachem of the Montauk Indians." Her words came slowly and quietly in hushed reverence:

"This place, our Land of the Rising Sun, your Big Shell Island, is the common birthplace for many of us gathered here today. And it was ever so for the ancestors of our ancestors and for the forefathers of your forefathers.

"We invite you to enter into peaceful negotiations with us. Sit with us in the sacred cave. Draw strength from its rocks. Harbor hope from its mystery of mysteries, its endless chain of circles. Let our mutual goodwill endure. Let our words of harmony extend to the setting sun and reach the skies. Banish those regrettable times when the islands of the Eastern Shores shook, when black clouds darkened the great waters.

"Today we kindle up a great council fire. We pray on the pipe of peace. We join hands in the chain of friendship. No evil spirit can break that circle.

"We return to you these islands, your Shell Islands, our Land of the Rising Sun. Let them pass on to all who wish to come to these friendly shores where fish swim and corn tassels blow in the breeze.

"We depart, but the memories of our people remain. The Great Spirit will roam these islands forever. The Great Mystery will shelter those who set foot in the shadows of the great cliffs. The Circle of Life will continue."

Matt and Annie gazed at each other in the moonlight. The beauty of the words and the strong emotions evoked left them speechless. They reached out to each other and held hands. A velvety cloak of silence enveloped them, muffling even the murmurs of the sea and wind.

The sudden sound of pebbles skittering across rocks broke the silence.

Annie extinguished her flashlight. "We have company," she whispered.

"Stay here," Matt said, "and don't make a sound." He slipped into the darkness.

Annie fumbled with her hair clip. She locked the chest. Instinctively, as if to protect a child, Annie wrapped the belt and deeds in the blanket and held them tightly in her arms. She flattened her back against the cliff and drew her knees to her chest, as if to disappear into the crevices. She heard breathing. Someone was crawling toward her. Closer and closer.

She rolled onto her stomach. Pushing the blanket in front of her, she crawled over the hole she and Matt had dug and elbowed her way into the cave. Her breath stabbed her throat. She crawled faster and faster, oblivious to the sharp walls and floor of the passage. A hand gripped her right ankle. She tried to pull free. A second hand grabbed her right calf. She pulled up her left knee and kicked with all her might.

"Ummph." The word echoed through the passage. She got him!

Fighting off panic, Annie struggled forward, groping her way through the slimy blackness. The arch, the flowstone. The floor sloping down, the leveling off. Finally the rim. She stood in the Dragon's Teeth, the blanket at her feet. She breathed hard, her flashlight poised, ready to strike her assailant.

Silence.

Dripping water.

Birds screeched.

"Aaaaaa!" Matt's painful cry echoed into the cave.

Matt. He'd been hurt!

Forgetting her own danger, Annie grabbed the blanket. She dropped to her hands and knees. She crawled out of the cave. She stood up and took a step. She tripped over something. A body.

"Matt, Matt, are you all right?" She shook his shoulders. She patted his face.

Matt sat up and groaned. He held his head. "I started to check the cave entrance when someone came at me from behind."

"Did you see who it was?"

"No."

"Was it a man or a woman?"

"I don't know. But whoever it was, they got the chest."

"But not the belt or deeds," Annie said. She put the blanket in Matt's hands and shined the flashlight on the back of his head. A nasty gash oozed blood. "Come on," she said, helping him to his feet. "Let's get back to camp and catch a thief."

Chapter Fifteen

Annie and Matt hurried toward camp. Just in case, Annie chose a route that was unfamiliar to the A-Team. A hoot owl screeched and flapped its wings. Annie stifled a scream. The wind picked up and whistled through the oak trees. Matt stopped, his muscles tense, ready to repel another attack.

Every sound, every movement, signaled danger. Annie clutched the blanket that held the deeds and wampum belt.

Halfway to camp, Matt staggered to a tree and rested against it. "I'm dizzy from that whack on the head."

"We'll rest here until you feel better."

"Go ahead without me," he insisted. "I'll catch up."

"Absolutely not." Annie placed her fists squarely on her hips.

"Come on, Annie. There's safety in numbers. At least two of the people at camp will help you. You're better off with them than with me."

"No," Annie said defiantly.

"Be reasonable. One of us has to return to camp as quickly as possible. We don't want to give the thief time to cover his tracks." He took a step forward, stumbled, and reached back to support himself on the tree.

Annie moved quickly to his side. "We shouldn't separate," she said. "Whoever hit you could still be out there waiting. And he knows you're hurt." Annie slid her arm around Matt's waist. "Lean on me," she said, and they set out again.

Slowly and anxiously, Annie helped Matt cross the jagged rocks and the tangled brush. Matt leaned heavily on Annie as they made their way across the bluffs. He stumbled several times and slipped and fell on the slick path where high grasses gave way to cattail marshes. Finally, they reached the slope that overlooked the beach.

Annie stopped abruptly. On the path in front of her lay the wooden chest. In the pale moonlight, she could see that the chest had been smashed. It was empty. "The thief knows we have the treasure," she whispered. The hair on the back of her neck rose.

Matt picked up the chest and ran his hand across the cracked side. "Who would do such a thing?" he asked.

"Until now I was convinced the thief was someone on the A-Team," Annie replied. For the first time, her voice trembled with fear. "But none of them would have harmed such an important archaeological find. Or thrown it away."

Matt wiped away the blood that oozed down his neck and into his collar. "Unless they were desperate." He cocked his head. "Shhh," he said. He kept perfectly still.

They waited. Silence.

"Let's get out of here," Annie whispered. "We're too vulnerable out here in the open."

Moving as quickly as Matt's condition allowed, they reached the scrub grasses that rimmed the knoll above camp. They crouched on their hands and knees and peered into the darkness, listening for sounds of trouble. They heard only the crackling twigs that smoldered in the campfire and the surf that battered the rocky shore.

Annie motioned Matt forward. They crawled toward camp. The sound of steady breathing assured them that each tent was occupied.

Matt pointed toward *Island Hoppers*. Annie nodded. They crept noiselessly across the sand.

"If someone on the A-Team is the thief, they're also a very good actor," Matt whispered when they had reached the dock.

"You're right," Annie replied. "Maybe they only pretend to be asleep until they can get their hands on the treasure."

"The treasure will be safer on *Island Hoppers* than in my tent or yours," Matt said.

Quickly and quietly, they lifted the forward and aft ropes from the dock pilings and climbed aboard. "We'll let her drift," Matt said. "Then we'll drop anchor when we've put some distance between us and the dock."

Annie hid the chest and the blanket in the box that contained the life preservers. "One more look," she said, "before we pack the treasure into watertight containers." She ran her fingertips across the sleek beads, following the glistening path of moonlight. Briskly, she rubbed her palms together. The power of the beads and the spirit world vibrated in her hands.

"You feel it too, don't you?" Matt asked. "The energy of shared trust."

"Yes," Annie said. "The shared trust between the Montauks and the white man, and between us." Gently, she rolled up the wampum belt. "A burden rests on our shoulders. We'll get the belt and deeds to the proper authorities, won't we, Matt?"

"We can make that happen, together," Matt answered.

As Annie nodded, a look of sadness fell across her face.

"What's the matter?" Matt asked, taking her in his arms.

The weariness, the worry and fear, everything, suddenly became too much for her. She hugged him tight. She needed to share her feelings and frustrations with someone. It was as if all the pieces of a puzzle were spread out on a table but at first she couldn't make them fit. And when they finally did fit, she couldn't understand the design.

"I was thinking about my parents," she began.

She took several deep breaths, and the words just tumbled out. "They tried to preserve the natural beauty of the Shell Island by keeping them part of the state park system. That may have cost them their lives. Gram thinks they were murdered. Their car tampered with. Their murderer is probably this same creep who's coming after us. Don't you see? We've got to find out who he is and stop him. For our own sake and for the memory of my parents."

Matt kissed Annie's forehead. "Don't worry. We'll get out of this and straighten everything out," he reassured her. "We'll go to the police. If necessary, we'll hire a private investigator to probe into your parents' deaths."

Annie sighed with relief. For the first time since the accident, a sense of calm, of purposefulness, filled her mind. Turning her face toward Matt's, she put her arms around his neck to kiss him. She pulled away quickly and looked at her hands. They were covered with the warm, sticky blood that had soaked into his collar and the back of his shirt.

"Matt. I'm sorry. Blabbing away like this. We need to take care of your wound. I'll go below and find the medicine kit."

"I'll take care of things topside," Matt said. Fighting nausea and dizziness, he placed the belt and deeds in one of the watertight containers Annie had brought back from Grayrocks. He gave the lid a final twist. Using his last ounce of energy, he dropped anchor and then stood back to survey the dock and shoreline for any sign of movement. Convinced that he and Annie were safe for the time being, he went below to the cabin.

"Lie down," Annie said. "Let's see the damage. If anyone comes along now, we can say you fell on the rocks at the beach." The flashlight beam found the wound. The cut was deeper and more serious than Annie had imagined. She washed the area with water, then dabbed it with an antiseptic solution.

"Gaaaah." Matt stifled a howl.

"You should see Doc Henderson when we get to Grayrocks." Worry and concern filled her voice. She bandaged the wound and was relieved when the bleeding stopped.

"Why see a doctor? I have my own medicine woman," Matt said weakly. He tried to stand, but he knocked his head against the low ceiling and sank to the floor.

"Rest here a minute until you get your bearings," Annie said, cradling his head in her lap.

Matt moaned and held his throbbing head. "The room's spinning," he said. His head lolled to the side. He was conscious, but his breathing was shallow.

Annie sang softly to herself "Hush little baby don't you cry." It was the go-away-nightmare lullaby she had relied on after the accident to keep away the scary shadow figures that hovered over her bed. *Please,* she thought, *don't let any harm come to us.*

She reached up and opened the cabin curtains. Moonlight flooded the room. She held Matt's head in the crook of her arm and stroked his head. She thought about the vacant sky above *Island Hoppers* and the bleak waters below. She and Matt were all alone, with no one to help them.

Trying to muster courage, she continued to sing, picking up the slap-slap-slide, slap-slap-slide rhythm of the waves rocking the boat. The words caught in her throat. Uncontrollable sobs escaped her lips. She closed her eyes and tried to conquer the growing panic that was spreading through her entire body. *Stay calm,* she told herself. *Matt will be all right. Dawn will come soon.*

As Annie and Matt waited for his dizziness to sub-side, a shadowy figure in a black wet suit crept along the dock. He descended the ladder and slipped into the water. He paddled a small, inflatable black raft toward *Island Hoppers.* Glistening in the moonlight, the slinky figure slithered up the anchor chain, glided over the railing, and stole aboard.

Annie's breath caught in her throat as the boat listed. There was a decided change in the rhythm of the rocking. She held her breath and waited, afraid to move. Then the familiar slap-slap-slide, slap-slap-slide reassuringly resumed.

Matt stirred, his eyelids fluttered. "What was that?"

"Nothing. A lull in the sea's rhythms. But I think

we'd better take turns standing guard. I'll go first. You need sleep."

Dazed and tired, Matt didn't argue. Before Annie left the room, Matt's eyes closed. His arm lay curled around the container that held the treasure.

Chapter Sixteen

Annie sat in the middle of the deck. She braced her back against the supporting pole of the brass banister that descended toward Matt's cabin. If anybody came, they wouldn't catch her off guard. She had seen too many movies in which the bad guys caught the hero unprepared, then bludgeoned him. Steeling herself for the worst, she gripped a hammer in one hand and a flashlight in the other.

The boat rocked in the swells of the choppy sea. Her eyelids drooped. Her chin bobbed toward her chest, then snapped up. She filled a bucket with water and set it by her side.

Minutes later, her chin snapped up again. She dipped her hand into the bucket and splashed cold water on her face. She had to stay awake. Her life and Matt's depended on keeping her eyes and ears open. The droplets glistened in the moonlight on her dark lashes. So did a shiny trail of small puddles that headed toward the prow.

The frogman crept along the deck. The whites of his eyes gleamed. He looked left and right. Smart to bide his time. Matt was belowdecks, asleep. The treasure was on the cot next to him. Annie was starting to doze. One push, she'd be overboard, and the treasure would be his.

Stay awake, Annie told herself. *Concentrate on something. The suspects. That's it. Think about the suspects. Dr. Winfield? He couldn't be the thief. The least impropriety, let alone an outright criminal act, would ruin his career. He's married to an Indian woman. His father-in-law, Donald Eagleton, would have spotted flaws in his character long ago.*

The frogman crept closer. The moon slid past its covering of black clouds. The frogman stopped short. He slithered sideways into the shadows.

Annie looked straight at the frogman but saw only blackness.

The frogman exhaled slowly. *Don't take stupid chances. Wait until her head drops forward.*

George and Ginny? Both were strong and physically capable of the attacks at the cave. But what would drive them to destroy or possibly sell the deeds and belt? Greed. Pure and simple greed. That had to be the motive, Annie decided.

The frogman crept closer. The wind was picking up. He didn't like the looks of the weather. Bad storm predicted. Annie had one minute; then he'd make his move.

A hired goon from the All-Atlantic Associates? The same one who tampered with her parents' car and sent it careening over the railing? Try as she might, she couldn't concentrate on the memories rolling around in her mind.

The frogman stepped from the shadows. He moved toward Annie. He raised his hands over his head.

Island Hoppers rolled and dipped violently. The storm that had threatened all day erupted with a vengeance. Rain splattered the deck. Wind roiled the water. *Island Hoppers* creaked and groaned.

The frogman slid. He caught himself on the railing and slunk back into the shadows.

Annie ducked for cover under a tarpaulin as thunder rumbled across the sky. *Forget the past,* she told herself. Matt, the belt, the deeds, and her own skin were her priorities. Huge swells crashed against *Island Hoppers*. Lightning flashed. In that split second of electrifying light, Annie saw the churning waves of the black sea.

Wait. Something else. There. Was she hallucinating? Was someone clutching the railing by the prow? She blinked several times.

A second flash of lightning. Eyes wide open. No one.

Before she could investigate, Matt appeared on the stairway, struggling into a hooded yellow slicker.

"Go below where it's dry. I'll stand watch." His voice carried above the sound of the waves that pounded the side of the boat. "Mother Nature's playing rough with us," he shouted, and fought to maintain his balance.

"Look on the bright side," Annie shouted. She squinted into the pelting rain that streaked her face. "We're safe from intruders." The image of a frogman jumped before her eyes. *Don't be stupid,* she told herself. *Don't start believing in tricks that tired eyes play.*

"Good," Matt shouted. "I'm not looking for another whack on the head. Or a dose of the medicine woman's antiseptic." They both laughed.

Sunlight streamed through the cabin window. Annie sat up. She yawned and stretched, forgetting for the moment where she was. She looked around. The container was gone. "Matt!" she called, and pulled on her jeans and shirt.

She and Matt almost crashed into one another on the stairs. "Someone's been here," he said, out of breath. "They snuck up behind me and held a cloth over my face. Chloroform, I think. I passed out."

"They came to the cabin too," Annie exclaimed. "They took the belt and deeds while I slept." She clenched her teeth. "This is out of control! We need to confront the A-Team. Are you up to it?"

Matt nodded.

"Good. Let's reclaim the missing treasure. Right now."

* * *

"We thought you were going to take off on *Island Hoppers* and leave us behind," Dr. Winfield said. He was crouched near the barbecue pit, scrubbing the grill. "Are you okay?" The furrows of his brow creased. "You both look terrible."

"We'll be fine once we find the thief who stole the treasure of Hidden Cave," Matt said.

"What treasure?" Dr. Winfield asked, dumbfounded. "You say the treasure's stolen. How do you know that?"

Ginny stopped dismantling the tents and glowered at Matt. "Are you accusing one of us?"

George set down the rappelling gear he was coiling. "Should I contact my lawyer?" he asked jokingly.

"That might be a good idea," Matt said.

Annie walked toward the piles of equipment and supplies ready to be loaded onto *Island Hoppers*. "Let's check every box and bag," she said to Matt.

"Can't this wait?" Ginny grumbled.

"Matt and I want to know right now," Annie said.

"Let me help," Dr. Winfield offered.

"Me too," George added.

"We'll handle this ourselves," Matt said.

Ignoring the A-Team's complaints, Matt and Annie pored through everything.

"Satisfied?" Ginny asked. Her pouty lips formed a faint smile, and her eyes narrowed.

"Not quite," Matt replied. "Dump everything out of your backpacks. You too, Dr. Winfield."

"I have nothing to hide," Dr. Winfield said. He scattered the contents of his pack on a blanket.

"Me, neither," George said, and turned his pack upside down.

"All right," Ginny complained. "But for the record, I don't like being treated like a common criminal." She picked up her pack, pulled back the flap, and yanked. A bottle of chloroform tumbled to the ground.

"Well, well," Annie said. "If it isn't little Miss Chemistry Expert, hard at work."

"So you're the one who chloroformed me," Matt said.

"I don't know how that chloroform got there," Ginny snapped. "And if this is someone's idea of a joke, it's not funny."

Matt picked up Ginny's pack and shook it. The belt fell out first, followed by the deeds.

"But . . . but . . . I've never seen these before," she stammered. "Someone else put them there."

Dr. Winfield fell to his hands and knees, overwhelmed by the magnificence and beauty of the belt. His hands trembled as he held the deeds and read them. He rocked back on his heels, his eyes closed, his face tilted toward the sun. "Never in my wildest dreams did I think we would find anything of such major importance." His voice cracked. "I can't wait for Donald to see these." He opened his eyes, and overcome with emotion, he staggered to his feet. "We'd better return to Grayrocks immediately and let the police resolve this," he said.

Ginny glared at everyone. Red blotches appeared on her freckled skin.

"Nice work, Ginny," Matt said, pointing toward his head wound.

"I don't know what you're talking about. George was the one skulking around in the middle of the night, not me." She turned and walked away.

Island Hoppers pulled into the Grayrocks marina. Gram, Tom, Sally, the entire group of Corner Cafe regulars, Matt's uncle David, Grayrocks's three police officers, and Hank, the chief of police, stood on the dock.

Ginny pushed forward. "What are the police doing here? How did they know there's been trouble?"

"My grandmother's on top of this situation. You can be sure of that," Annie said proudly.

Hank stood on one foot, his other leg bent behind him, resting on the dock piling. He looked like a blue flamingo. He worked his toothpick to the side of his mouth and ambled to the edge of the dock. "Stand back and let my boys in blue do their job." His arms moved up and down away from his sides in quick birdlike motions. His beady eyes surveyed the group on the dock as if they were a flock of unruly crows that intended to surge forward and knock him into Grayrocks Bay.

Hank moved his arms forward in a semicircle, as if to embrace Annie, Matt, and the A-Team as they stepped off *Island Hoppers*. He eyed the dock crowd one more time. "Nobody say nothing until I'm done with my official interrogation." He clenched his teeth and spit the words out like bullets.

Annie read the body language and facial expressions of the assembled group. Sally, who had "I'm glad to see you" written all over her face, stopped wiping her hands nervously on her apron and waved to Annie.

The cafe regulars leaned left, then right, hooking their thumbs under their chins and covering their mouths with their splayed fingers as they whispered their opinions to their neighbors.

Gram gave Annie a thumbs-up signal fortified with a V-for-victory sign.

Tom crossed his arms over his chest, seemingly proud of some accomplishment or other.

David Revington craned his neck, checking out Matt's bloodstained shirt, obviously concerned about his nephew's well-being.

The boys in blue? Well—Annie chuckled to herself—they were acting like the Boys in Blue. Moving with a calculated slowness, they addressed the crowd with a formality reserved for those rare occasions when they did more than hand out parking tickets. They dropped words from the corners of their mouths like "perpetrator" . . . "DNA" . . . "and alleged crime scene."

Annie locked eyes with Matt. He shrugged his shoulders as if to say, *What's going on?*

Annie saw Mr. Downing, owner, photographer, and chief reporter for the *Grayrocks Gazette,* lean forward to snap several pictures. Predicting the sequence of events, he marched in front of the crowd like a drum major at the Fourth of July parade. He led them past the firehouse and town square toward the Grayrocks Police Station.

Annie had to admit that the town of Grayrocks had a style all its own when it came to sorting out mysteries.

Chapter Seventeen

The next evening, Annie and Matt sat across from Tom and Sally at Gram's kitchen table. From her perch at the head of the table Gram said, "Tom, I made that potato salad especially for you. . . . Annie, don't leave any coleslaw in that bowl . . . Sally, the beans are getting cold." She squirted lemon on her flounder. "Matt, I insist you have seconds of the fish. Don't fight me on this."

"No, thanks," Matt said, patting his stomach. "I'm saving room for your blueberry pie."

Annie realized how much Matt appreciated a down-home style of living. As far as she could see, he had never enjoyed the elegant life he had known in his posh New York City surroundings. Maybe that's why he had moved west and taken up racing. Did that explain his attraction to her? Maybe she was merely part of his desire to escape his parents and their stuffy lifestyle. Where did she fit into his life now, she wondered. He intended to leave Grayrocks to pursue his career. He couldn't make any commitment about their future together. Cars were his first and only love.

Tom chuckled and turned to Matt. "I don't know if the town can handle the excitement of all that's happened since you and Annie returned to Grayrocks with the wampum belts and deeds. That was really something, Hank marching all of you—the Famous Five—down to the station."

"Tom and I stood on the on the garage cans in the alley," Gram interjected. "We saw and heard everything through the broken window."

"What a sight." Tom's smile spread to a broad grin. "Matt, you should have seen yourself and Annie, shifting on those hard chairs across from George, Ginny, and Dr. Winfield. Hank paced, his shoes squeaking like they needed a lube job. Pete, Charlie, and Joe stood with their arms folded across their chests trying to look like important investigating officers. Each guarded a separate wall of the room as if someone intended to steal the plaster."

Sally said, "Well, I wasn't there. And Tom's been too busy blabbing away to everyone in Grayrocks except me. I've heard the drift. Can somebody fill in the details?"

Matt wiped his mouth with the back of his hand. "We can credit George's father with getting things under way. According to him, some tough guys had been calling and threatening to go to the Shells and rough up George . . . or worse. Seems like George's gambling debts finally caught up with him. The father knew nothing about George's poker habit, but he didn't like the threats. So he called the chief of the Grayrocks police to check up on his son. Well, you can imagine how Hank cooperated with an outsider. That's when George's father sent out two of his vice presidents to see what was what."

Tom laughed heartily. "Gram worked her magic on those big shots in creased pants when they stayed at the inn. She found out they were okay guys, interested in locating George for his own good. Her cooking, especially those second helpings of bourbon cake, knocked the stuffing out of them fellas. They slept until noon." He slapped his knee. "Kept them away from Big Shell Island and from complicating matters for Annie and Matt."

"I still can't believe George got in over his head like that," Annie said. "He had told the tough guys he was about to get his hands on something valuable. Something that would more than pay off his gambling debts. They pressed him hard, and he told what he knew about the buried treasure. He even paid an artist to draw a wampum belt similar to one in a research book. That drawing convinced the tough guys that a belt did exist."

Matt said, "When confronted by the police, George cooperated fully. This morning he led Hank to the hidden raft and frogman suit that he had used the night he stole the treasure." Matt rubbed the back of his head. "I forgot to thank George for trying to knock some sense into my thick head. He really had me fooled. I could've sworn he was asleep in the tent. Dr. Winfield must've been snoring loud enough for two."

Gram sighed contentedly. "Everything worked out."

Annie added, "Even with Ginny. She didn't stay mad at us for accusing her. She was too busy impressing the boys in blue. Said she loves a man in uniform."

"I love happy endings," Sally said dreamily as she set down her glass of iced tea.

"Dr. Winfield sure is one very happy man," Matt said. "He's going to publish the findings and bring glory to Andrews University. Ginny's happy, too. She'll assist Dr. Winfield and share in the honors."

"And Long Island will get some well-deserved recognition," Gram said. She hopped off her chair and began clearing away the plates. "The Northport Museum has invited Donald Eagleton to kick off the opening exhibition of the belt and deeds with a ritual drama. And speaking as the president of S.O.S., you can rest assured that the Shell Islands will remain part of the park system."

Gram began dunking the pans in sudsy water. "Best of all, the Tourism Bureau of Grayrocks, that would be Mayor Tim Jones and his wife, Dolly, have dollar signs in their eyes. They predict that their new brainstorm, ecotourism, will bring in a whole new bunch of visitors. Can't you see them? All that chino and earth tones. It's enough to make you long for the return of splashy touristy colors."

Gram patted the guests' memory book on the buffet. "I may have to turn those unfinished rooms over the garages into more tourist quarters."

"Even George is part of the happy ending," Matt said as he began loading the dishwasher. "For turning over the names of the tough guys, he'll avoid prosecution. The court requires him to do community service and attend weekly gambling-addiction counseling but no hard time in jail."

Annie scooped the leftover food into containers. "Your father and uncle must be pleased," she said to Matt. "The Revington name will now be respected in Grayrocks."

Matt wrung out the sponge. "Those guys who threatened to rough up George? They were found through phone records, and they cut a deal with the FBI. All-Atlantic Associates had hired them. They rolled over names and dates of All-Atlantic Associates's shady land deals."

Matt wrapped one arm around Annie and the other around Gram. "And they admitted that the guy who threatened Caitlin and Andy and then tampered with their car, intentionally causing their deaths, worked for All-Atlantic Associates. Those unsavory land developers had feared Caitlin and Annie five years ago. Since then, they've followed all Save Our Shells committee activities. When they got wind of the A-Team's expedition, they checked out each member's habits. George's gambling was a breakthrough for them. They found out about the treasure. They would have destroyed it if they'd had the chance."

"There's only one matter left unresolved," Gram said. The two lines between her eyes deepened. "Caitlin and Andy's murderer has eluded the police. I want him brought to justice and thrown in the slammer."

"That will happen," Matt reassured her. "FBI agents are on his trail. Don't worry, Gram. All-Atlantic Associates will save their own hides. The word around town is that All-Atlantic Associates will hunt down the murderer and give him up. In return, the FBI will forgive and forget some of All-Atlantic Associates sleazy deeds."

Gram squeezed Matt's hand. "Something good came of Caitlin and Andy's deaths. I have to believe that."

"Of course it did," Sally said, rolling up the table-cloth. "The Shell Islands will be preserved for future generations."

"Caitlin and Andy are gone." Gram's voice faltered. "But my Annie has been set free. She realizes now that she couldn't have dragged her parents from the car and saved them."

Annie hugged Gram. "Lucky for me, Gram is patient and downright persistent. She told me over and over, 'Forgive yourself for surviving.' "

Annie looked up into Matt's eyes. "I think I'm ready now to go forward with my life."

"The murderer will be found," Sally said. "Never give up hope that things will work out right. That's one thing I've learned in the past year." She kissed Tom's cheek.

Tom said, "And I've finally learned about the importance of family . . . and friends." He mock-wrestled with Matt. "Make sure you come back this winter. We'll go iceboating with the guys. You ain't seen nothing til you see us drag them old stern-steerers to the frozen ponds. Sails billowing, we hurtle across the ice at fifty miles an hour. The brandy-laced coffee ain't bad, either."

Iceboating? Matt had really been accepted, Annie decided. Usually, it took a generation or two before an outsider was welcomed. Matt was the exception to the rule.

Sally looked at her watch. "The sitter has to be home by midnight." She and Tom shifted from one foot to the other, awkward as teenagers at the Grayrocks prom.

Gram said softly, "I'll say good night."

Annie turned to Matt. "How about a walk down by the bay?" She hoped the darkness of the night would conceal her tears. She knew that Matt would soon be leaving Grayrocks. He would pursue his dream of being a race-car driver. The sadness of the moment engulfed her, and she thought her heart would break.

Chapter Eighteen

Annie and Matt walked in the warm evening air, their arms encircling each other's waist. Moonlight skimmed the beads of water that clung to the grass and sidewalks. Grayrocks had never looked prettier, Annie thought. And Matt had never looked more handsome. She marveled at his rugged profile, the high cheekbones of his Indian forefathers.

"Let's go this way," Matt said, steering her toward the marina. "There's something on board *Island Hoppers* I want to show you."

He sounded so mysterious. What could it be?

They arrived at the marina dock where Harry, the night guard, strolled among the boats. Music played softly from his radio. Harry nodded and continued his rounds.

The night breezes brought in the salty scents of

181

crab pots and oyster beds. Off in the distance, the waves of the open water crashed against the rocks between Grayrocks Harbor and the deep channel. Fish nibbled at the reflections of lights bobbing on the surface. They sent circling ripples that merged and drifted in dizzying patterns.

Annie remembered all those warm summer nights when she and her parents had walked to the dock carrying their pails of bait and dropped their fishing lines into the silky blackness. How special she had felt then. As if she and her parents were the only three people in the world—safe, happy, indestructible. Standing close to Matt, their arms touching, she felt that same sensation. Contentment seeped through every pore of her body. It was the remembered contentment of a young girl who could not even imagine what a wily, unpredictable place the world was.

"I'm glad we had this summer, Annie. We went through a lot together." He put his arm around her shoulder and pulled her close. "But there could have been more."

"I wasn't interested in a summer fling, Matt."

"Me, either."

He saw the tears glistening on her lowered lashes. "So we'll let tomorrow come and never see each other again? Is that what you want?"

She turned her face toward Matt's and kissed him tenderly. "I'll never forget you."

"It doesn't have to end here. You'll finish college and become a famous illustrator. I'll make my mark in the racing world, and then . . ."

"And then?" The cruelty of those two words hit Annie. Tears spilled onto her cheeks.

"There's a future for us here in Grayrocks." Matt clasped Annie in his arms and led her out on the dock. They began to dance across the wooden planks, slow and easy. Time seemed to stop, willing to surrender one final hour. Annie rested her head on Matt's chest. He released his firm grip on her hand and drew her close, linking his hands at the small of her back. She felt secure and incredibly happy in his embrace. He moved with the same grace and ease with which he had scaled the walls of Hidden Cave.

Annie felt the muscles in his back, the same ones she had drawn that day on the beach. She followed his lead, forward, backward, circling, her body close to his. She was too happy to speak or even think about living her life without him.

"I should have thought of slow dancing a long time ago," he whispered. "I finally found a way to hold you in my arms without your running away."

Annie wanted to remember every detail of this night forever. She looked at the silver of moon that balanced on the marina rooftop. Moonbeams spread a silver carpet across the black waters, melding the sky and the bay, encircling the boats rocking gently against the dock. Annie drank up the moonlight until she was so full she thought she would burst. She felt transported. She saw herself and Matt, infinitesimal specks in a vast universe, yet an integral part of it, sheltered in the all-encompassing embrace of the immense sea and boundless sky.

Annie drew Matt closer. She kissed him. Dancing beneath the stars, Annie Devane knew she would love Matt Revington for all eternity. She wanted him more than she had ever wanted anything in her entire life.

Matt bent down and kissed Annie on the lips. He stopped dancing and stood perfectly still, hugging her tightly to his chest. "Marry me," he whispered in her ear. She couldn't bring herself to break free of his embrace. Matt did that for her. Slowly, he released her. His eyes never left her face. He stepped back, silhouetted against the star-filled sky, and held her at arm's length. "Marry me," he repeated.

"What about college . . . and racing?" she stammered.

"They're in our plans. You'll illustrate award-winning books. I'll win some races. And then we'll get married and live happily ever after in Grayrocks."

She leaned forward and kissed him on the mouth. She savored the warmth of his lips, the feelings that surged through her body whenever they kissed. She felt such a deep and abiding love for Matt that at times she wondered what her life had been like before she met him.

Matt took Annie's hand and helped her board *Island Hoppers.* "I want you to meet the future owner of the marina."

"Who?"

"Me," Matt said proudly. "Uncle David has decided to give up boats and devote himself full-time to golf and tennis. He's buying the East Bay Country Club. A year or so from now, I'll take over the marina."

Annie was speechless.

"Oh, I almost forgot." He reached down and picked up a small blanket wrapped around a bundle. "I have something for you."

"What's this?" she asked, taking the bundle from him.

"Open it and find out."

She sat down and carefully rolled back the edges of the blanket. Wampum beads glistened like amethysts and pearls in the moonlight. "Matt, it's beautiful," she said, running her fingers over the strings of purple beads with four inserts of white beads.

"It's a Montauk courtship string," he said. "Donald thought I might find a use for it. So how about it?"

"How about what?"

"Marrying me and living in Grayrocks," he said.

"But Matt—" He kissed her. "There are so many obstacles," she said.

His gaze was steady, his voice sexy. He held her so tight she could hardly breathe. "We could have a good life here, Annie. With your talent, you'll have more work than you can handle."

She had only to trust him, to say yes and she'd have exactly what she wanted. "Yes, Matthew Revington. With all my heart, yes. I love you. I'll marry you."

She threw her arms around his neck. They held each other close.

"You've just made all my dreams come true," he said, and Annie smiled. Matt had taken her thoughts and spoken them out loud.